Amor Proibido—
Forbidden Love

Gilda Arruda

PublishAmerica
Baltimore

First printing

ISBN: 1-60703-139-6
PUBLISHED BY PUBLISHAMERICA, LLLP
www.publishamerica.com
Baltimore

Printed in the United States of America

Dedicated to all of the sacrificing mothers of the world.

Author's Note

The sweeping changes that modernized post-World War I Europe did not affect the antiquated villages of Portugal. In the 1920s, it was still the traditional custom to arrange marriages. Because of this, few women ventured outside their native villages. The men, however, often left to escape the harsh realities of village life in search of making a better living in the more explored territories.

Women were viewed as property, not equals, and this narrow-minded treatment limited women's rights to almost nothing. What few claims to freedom these women made were immediately forbidden and taken away. Yet some still managed to hold fast to their identities, to thrive despite the oppressive demands their men and their society imposed on them. This is the story of one such woman.

Chapter 1

"I am sick and tired of hearing whispers that I'm already an old maid!" Ana cried.

Valentina knew Ana unconsciously felt unworthy. The muttered truths about Ana's mother were almost too much to bear. Valentina thought it was always better to placate her friend when she was in one of her moods. "It's not that bad," she offered lamely.

"Not that bad? I hear the old women scoffing! They say my mother must have angered the gods. 'Poor thing,' they mock, 'who does she take after?' Do you know how that makes me feel?" Ana could feel the tears threatening to spill, but she held herself in check. She refused to cry over the old crones of the village and their false opinions of her.

No one ever noticed the neat, meticulous way Ana kept her clothes and her person, or the perfect bun without a hair out of place, held together by her grandmother's ivory comb, one of her few prized possessions. They refused to focus on the air of quiet dignity that surrounded her. Instead, some of the villagers poked fun at her outward appearance, as well as her lineage. They would not acknowledge that a bastard child could be of any use in their simple little part of the world.

Valentina shook her head at Ana's distress. "Why do you let them affect you this way? What about your secret dreams about the wonderful man who will one day rescue you from those vicious stone-throwers?"

Ana looked over at her friend. It was easy for Valentina to dismiss the villagers and their antiquated ways. Her daring attitude, combined with her perfect looks, caused everyone in the village to treat Valentina much better than they would ever treat Ana. Valentina's long, honey-colored, wavy hair was the envy of her many admirers and a source of pride and rebellion. Where Ana was often considered ordinary, Valentina was called exceptional. "My dream man is just that, a dream. No one will ever come and take me from here. Once they see you, they'll forget all about me." Ana knew she was no match for the affections of the boys in the village. Her own black hair seemed too rich for her olive skin and did not match her somber brown eyes. She was too plain and too serious for anyone in the village to notice her.

Valentina's throaty laugh echoed in the little garden where they sat. "That's your problem, Ana. You refuse to think any big dreams for yourself. Look at me. Sure, I have many prospects of marriage, or at least that's what my mother says, but I have other ideas. My man will be rich and successful. He will own much land and animals and give me the lifestyle I dream of. You have to think the same way if you ever want to get out of here."

"I don't know how to be more like you," Ana admitted. Although older by several years, Ana followed in Valentina's shadow. Sometimes she thought Valentina took pity on her because she was so reserved and had no other friends, but she did not mind. Ana's shell would show its cracks when Valentina made light of her serious nature. Instead of being a torment as with the villagers, Valentina's teasing and silly pranks seemed to show Ana a side of herself she did not know existed. "Maybe I'll practice," she added with a smile.

"Perfect!" Valentina stood up and dusted off her dress. "Now let's go down to the fruit orchard and borrow some oranges from the sour-faced old woman with the two protruding front teeth. After all," Valentina concluded, "it's only over the hill, and surely the old woman must be napping by now."

"You mean steal," Ana corrected her as she also stood up. It was on days like this one that Ana felt completely free from the sadness of her existence. She was no longer surprised at Valentina's boldness. She had become used to her sudden impulses, as well as Ana's role as the dutiful accomplice. She meekly followed Valentina up the hill to bring home Queen, the family goat that had been out grazing. Valentina led Queen down to the barn and put her away, then shielded her eyes against the sun. "It's still early," she said. "We have time to go borrow, not steal, our oranges."

Ana wanted to protest, but she knew it would be useless. Valentina simply grabbed her hand and dragged her along. They again climbed the hill, laughing and joking as they stopped to survey the plots of land below. The old woman and her workers were nowhere in sight. Valentina smiled in anticipation and continued to pull Ana along.

"One of these days you are going to get us into serious trouble," Ana predicted.

Valentina paused and let out a dramatic sigh. "Getting caught does not faze me, o serious, worrisome Ana. It only makes me more determined to succeed."

They ventured down the other side of the hill. As they walked towards the valley, they slowed their pace as they took in the sight of the rising, pale smoke from the oven fires. It was a sure sign of the supper meal. Valentina was so caught up in her observations that she suddenly lost her footing and tumbled backwards. She tried to regain her balance, but her wooden clogs were no match for the slippery grass. Ana froze as Valentina stumbled down the small but bumpy hill. Valentina shot out her hand to try and grab onto Ana, but only managed to drag her down the hill as well. They landed in a heap at the bottom, bruised and overflowing with laughter at their clumsiness.

"You have no one to blame but yourself," Ana teased as she brushed bits of grass off her dress.

"Maybe if I'd had your sensible shoes I wouldn't have slipped," Valentina shot back. Ana looked stricken for a moment, and then joined in her friend's merriment. It was no secret that Ana's good grooming and expensive clothes were the result of her mother's well-paying occupation.

They were laughing so hard that they never heard the old woman approach them. She grabbed hold of Valentina's arm before the girls had a chance to run away and spat out, "Haven't I told you to stay away from my oranges!"

The look of stark terror on Ana's face was all Valentina needed to step forward and offer her services in exchange for a pardon. "I will clean your house for two weeks if you don't tell our mothers." Although Valentina put on a brave face for Ana's sake, secretly she prayed, *Please God, help me get out of this one.* She knew God was listening because the old woman eased her grip just enough that Valentina pulled away and fled with Ana in tow. She'd been down this road with the old woman enough times to know that only a day's worth of cleaning was necessary to keep her quiet until the next time Valentina was unfortunate enough to get caught.

Their escape was cut short by the arrival of three uniformed soldiers. It was not unusual to see soldiers walking through the villages, but their presence in the orchard came as a shock. Valentina's shock turned to embarrassment, however, as she realized the soldiers were openly gawking at them in silent amusement. She instantly assessed her appearance. If Ana was any indication of how she herself must look, then they had to get out of there quickly. She managed to lean in and whisper to Ana as she pulled a stray leaf out of her tangled hair, "It's going to be extremely difficult to compose ourselves. Just follow me." Valentina raised her head high, took Ana's hand, and to the horror of the old woman, grabbed two oranges off a nearby tree. They strolled to the back door of the old woman's house, headed straight down the hallway and left through the front door.

"That was close!" Valentina paused for a minute and tried to straighten her hair. She took a swift look around and immediately stopped her primping. In her haste to run away from the old woman and the soldiers, she had forgotten they were no longer in the poor section of the village. As she walked by the well-kept houses and tidy yards overflowing with multicolored hydrangeas, rich green ferns, and fragrant rainbow-colored roses, the shocking reality that she was out of her element could not have been more obvious when she saw Dimitri Maciel leaning against his front porch, talking to a friend. Their eyes met for a brief moment, but she looked away before anyone else could notice.

"Don't look now," Ana whispered, "but Dimitri is standing over there. I didn't realize we were passing his house." Ana stole a glimpse at him to see if he was watching them. Although he appeared deep in conversation, his eyes kept straying to the disheveled pair.

"I know," Valentina replied. "I must look a mess. Of all the days to see him!" She unconsciously straightened her skirt as she kept walking.

Even at a distance, Dimitri recognized Valentina's distinctive walk with the graceful glide that was hers alone. "Valentina!" Dimitri shouted just as she thought they were in the clear. He ran up and flashed a grin at her. "Did you lose that lazy pig Jorge again?" he asked with a devilish smile.

"We were picking oranges," Ana broke in, "and we lost our footing and fell down the hill."

Valentina was about to deliver a swift kick to Ana's shin when Dimitri said, "I've already told you Valentina, I'll swap you an orange for a kiss any time you want. My oranges are much sweeter than that sour-faced old lady's."

With her head held high, Valentina said matter-of-factly, "I'll keep that in mind for next time." She tossed her hair back over her shoulder and smiled up at him. "Let's go, Ana." She took Ana's arm a little too forcefully and they proceeded down the street.

"Why didn't you take him up on his offer and go pick oranges from his trees? Could it be that you like him too? Why are you shaking so much?" Ana asked a little too innocently.

"Because," Valentina replied, annoyed that she was reacting this way over Dimitri Maciel, "his class doesn't mix with the likes of us."

Ana could see the sheen of unshed tears in her eyes. "Where he is well-learned and educated," Valentina continued, "I can't even spell my own name. Besides," she added as she wiped her eyes with the back of her hand, "I'd rather work for my oranges than take a gift from him. I don't need Dimitri's pity." They walked the rest of the way home in silence.

Grateful no one was home, Valentina went into her backyard and sat under the big birch tree. It was her favorite place to spend some quiet time by herself and play her guitar. She started to carefully fold the towels in the basket at her feet so her mother wouldn't get upset over the wrinkles she usually left in them, but the more she thought of today's events, the messier the towels looked. Why did she let Dimitri Maciel get to her?

She considered this as she peeled one of the oranges she took from Sour Face that afternoon. Dimitri was just a man after all, although an extremely handsome one. She'd known him for years, had played with him as a child despite their obvious class differences. But lately he stirred a different feeling in her, one that moved beyond friendship into something she wasn't sure she understood.

The orange peels fell to the ground unnoticed as Valentina wondered about his feelings for her. He teased her mercilessly. Did he even see her as anything but the poor housekeeper's daughter? The thought made her cringe. Despite the respect the village showed her mother, the fact that they were poor and without a man at home did not go unnoticed, and tongues had often wagged over her absent father's sudden departure. What would Dimitri ever see in someone like her?

"I don't know what I was thinking," she muttered as she took a bite of her orange. They really weren't sweet, after all.

* * *

Dimitri strolled into the house and deposited himself on one of his mother's expensive dining room chairs. He took in his surroundings, realizing for the first time that he'd never paid attention to the decor of this room before. The furnishings were tasteful and luxurious, a testament to his father's position in the village. Dr. Maciel took good care of his family, but the wealth around them could not make up for the cold, insensitive way his parents regarded each other. He hoped he would never treat the woman he loved with such low regard.

And who might that be? His conscience mocked. His thoughts immediately went to Valentina, her dirt-streaked face and tangled web of hair the most beautiful sight he'd seen the whole day. He smiled as he remembered the rebellion in her eyes as she'd casually tossed aside his remark about the oranges, and the way she carried herself as she dragged her poor, defenseless sidekick Ana away with her. He'd taken one look into those deep, moss green eyes and been lost. He wanted her as he'd never wanted anything in his life. But she never made a secret of the fact that they came from different sections of the village, she from the poorest section, and he from the upper, well-to-do part of the village, and she reminded him of that every chance she got. But there was only so much rejection a man could take, he reflected as he rose from his seat and headed for his room. He would wait for the right moment to declare his feelings for her. "I'm a patient man," Dimitri chuckled as he closed the dining room door behind him. "I will prove her wrong."

Chapter 2

Valentina stayed out of the old woman's orchard for two weeks after the last incident. She instead devoted most of her free time to her favorite passion, her music. It was well known in the village that Valentina not only played the guitar as well as any professional musician, but she had the voice to go with it. She would spend hours composing songs just for the sheer joy of it, and it was in the middle of one of these impromptu performances in her back yard that Ana happened to find her.

"Valentina! I need to talk to you." Ana entered the small yard and sat down across from her friend.

Valentina placed her guitar at her side and said, "This better be good Ana. I was practicing for Sunday."

"It is, trust me. Do you remember the soldiers we saw in the old woman's field a few weeks ago?" Ana's eyes had taken on a dreamy quality, and Valentina rolled her own. Obviously, Ana was smitten with one of them. "One of them was asking about you all over the village the other day. The handsome one."

She didn't even remember who she'd seen that day. All soldiers looked alike to her, handsome or not. "That's nice," she replied. The last person Valentina wanted to get mixed up with was a soldier. "But I have to practice. I don't have time to sit and daydream about some soldier in the village." She retrieved her guitar and strummed a few chords. "I'll be singing in the village square Sunday after mass, and I want to make sure I sound perfect."

"What if he comes here looking for you? Are you going to turn him away?" Ana turned to look at the gate, as if by mentioning him the soldier would magically appear.

"I'm not interested in him," Valentina insisted. "If you like him so much, you go find him yourself."

"I do not like him!" Ana protested, but a deep blush suddenly stained her cheeks.

"You're a terrible liar, Ana. We'll see if he comes around. If he does, maybe I can play matchmaker." Valentina smiled at her closest friend, but it did not quite reach her eyes. She wanted to see Ana happy and wed. The village women were so cruel and unforgiving towards her that it broke her heart to see Ana take their abuse and not be able to do a thing about it. If this soldier could bring a light into Ana's life, she would do what she could to help it along.

"Thank you Valentina! Do you really think he will come by?" Ana asked eagerly as she hugged her friend and got ready to leave.

"I think so. Not to worry, he'll fall in love with you in no time," she promised, but a small voice in the back of her mind suggested otherwise. The soldier was looking for *her* in the village, not Ana, yet she did not want anything to do with him. She would try her best to bring them together, but the small instinctive voice warned that it would not be as she wished. She shook off her dark thoughts and resumed playing, the melancholy notes of an old ballad filling the air.

* * *

Dimitri Maciel blew out a puff of smoke as he watched and listened to Valentina strum her guitar behind the safety of her gate. He dropped the half-smoked cigarette on the ground and crushed it with his right foot, then shoved his hands in his pants pockets and started for home. Part of him wanted to run straight through the gate and kiss her, but he was a patient man. He would wait until she was ready.

The streets were empty at this time of day, with most of the men in the village at home eating lunch before they headed back to the fields for the rest of the day's work. He did not have those concerns, however. His father made enough money to keep Dimitri in cigarettes and his hands clean from the dirt of the fields. It was one of the things Valentina resented about him, and she was often quick to point out his other faults as well. She thought that at twenty-two, he was more than capable of earning his own bread. But something about that girl drew him to her, and the feelings she provoked at once disturbed and intrigued him. But she was not in his social class, a fact his mother was constantly reminding him of. It did not seem to matter to anyone in his family how he felt. All that mattered was the Maciel family name.

As he reached the edge of the "poor" section of the village, he spotted a young soldier speaking to Ana, Valentina's sidekick. *She's got herself a beau,* he mused, a little surprised because the poor girl's reputation was worthless as far as the villagers were concerned. He kept walking, noting that the soldier wasn't really listening to Ana. He caught snatches of their conversation, and heard Valentina's name mentioned. Jealousy flared through him as he understood that the soldier was not interested in Ana after all, but was looking for Valentina. He would have to keep a close eye on this situation, Dimitri realized as he crossed onto his own street and headed home.

* * *

Ana practically floated back into Valentina's yard. "I saw him!" she declared as she made herself comfortable on a small bench.

Valentina made a face at her and kept playing. "Has he proposed yet?" she teased.

"No, of course not! He asked me where you live, and if he could call on you. I guess he really wants to meet you." Ana suddenly looked very sad, and Valentina reached out a hand and patted her shoulder.

"Maybe he's shy and rather have me here as a chaperone. You know we aren't supposed to be out alone with anyone. I would have to accompany you." The lie rolled easily off her tongue. Taking a deep breath, Valentina pushed onward. "If he comes by in the next few days, we'll entertain him, and see what his intentions are."

"You're sure you have no interest in him?" Ana asked. "You'll help me win him?"

"Absolutely! I don't want anything to do with him." The little voice begged to be heard, but Valentina pushed the thought away. She had no intentions of getting involved with a soldier. Her rich, successful man was out there somewhere, and she would be waiting for him when he at last arrived.

The next two days flew by with no visits from the soldier, and Valentina assumed he'd lost interest in calling on her. She breathed a sigh a relief as she waited in the backyard for Ana. While she wondered about the soldier's intentions, her thoughts kept straying to Dimitri.

Dimitri Maciel was a contradiction to her, and he had been since their childhoods. He could be charming and sweet, but at the same time he was lazy and arrogant. He thought a little too much of himself and not enough of her. At least that's what

Valentina believed. He teased her mercilessly but never made any intentions known to her of his feelings towards her or otherwise. She waited for a sign she had no hope of ever receiving. Their lives were so different, as if a great chasm separated them. She was poor, had no dowry, and no hopes of ever marrying someone like Dimitri. And he was far too concerned with himself to ever notice her anyway. He teased her because he thought it was funny to pick on her as he had when they were little, not because he cared for her. In her heart she knew there was no chance for them, but she secretly hoped so.

Her chaotic thoughts were interrupted by Ana's arrival. "He's coming this afternoon!" she beamed as she plopped down on the grass. Valentina noticed that Ana had on one of her church dresses, and her grandmother's comb adorned the immovable bun she always wore. As always, the sensible shoes completed her outfit, and Valentina smiled. "You seem prepared."

"I went to the market for cheese and saw him buying food. I overheard him tell the shopkeeper that it was for a picnic with his intended," she admitted. Ana never eavesdropped, unlike Valentina, who would ask someone to repeat what they'd said if she'd heard incorrectly. *Ana must be very taken with this man if she's stooping to my tactics,* Valentina concluded.

"It's not like you to listen to other people's conversations, Ana. I'm surprised at you!" At the pained look on Ana's face, Valentina laughed. "Look there, is that him?" She pointed to a uniformed man walking across the street towards the house, a large basket in one hand. He smiled as he approached the gate, but did not let himself in. He asked in a clear, deep voice, "May I enter, Valentina? My name is Antonio Fero, and your friend Ana said I could call on you sometime this week."

"Did she really?" Valentina glanced over at Ana, who looked ready to faint. "Permission to come calling has to be asked for and granted, but because you've come a long way, and for that reason only, we will speak to you out here, but only for a few minutes."

Feeling defeated, he said, "As you wish. I will sit here." He indicated the space next to Ana, and for a moment, Valentina thought he might actually be here for her friend. The thought relaxed her somewhat, and she took a seat in front of them both.

"Tell us about yourself, Antonio. Ana did not say much about you." Valentina eyed the basket. It was well past lunch, and she realized she was very hungry.

Antonio began to empty the contents of the basket. He'd brought bread, cheese, oranges, and a canister of fresh milk. "I only met Ana briefly the other day. We did not talk long, but she said I was welcome to come by and visit." He opened the milk, and Valentina rose to get three mugs. She hesitated before she reached for the chipped and mismatched mugs. Valentina shook her head at her family's poverty, but she picked up the mugs and headed outside. When she returned, she could see how much Ana liked Antonio; she sat at rapt attention, taking in every word he said. Valentina approached the pair, placing the mugs on the ground before she sat down. Antonio poured out milk for each of them, and then passed the bread and cheese. "I thought I might ask a little about you," he said as he offered Valentina an orange. For some strange reason, she could not explain, the thought of taking it from him felt offensive. "No thank you," she said, and she put the fruit back in the basket.

"But I thought…never mind." They ate in silence for a time, each caught up in their own thoughts. Valentina's earlier impression of Antonio had been replaced with a nagging suspicion. He paid no attention to Ana at all. She sat by his feet, nearly drooling over every word he said, yet he did not seem to notice she was even there. Something had to be done, Valentina thought.

"Antonio, did you know that Ana is an excellent embroiderer?" Valentina finished off her bread and smiled at her friend. "She's also a wonderful cook."

Antonio looked over at Ana as if seeing her for the first time. "Those are excellent qualities to have." He then turned his attention to Valentina. "And what do you like to do?"

The afternoon passed in this fashion. Ana tried desperately to include herself in the conversation, but Antonio always managed to maneuver his questions back to Valentina. For her part, she wished he would just leave. She had had enough of his flattery. She did note, however, that he claimed to be rather wealthy, and had a large spread of land in a nearby village. Other than that, there was not much about Antonio to endear him to her. He wasn't nearly as handsome as Dimitri. His short stature and dark looks lent him an untrustworthy air. Valentina wasn't sure what about him attracted Ana so much. He simply felt wrong to her, though she didn't know why.

The sun began to set when he finally left the girls. Valentina watched as he strolled down the street, the now empty basket hanging on one arm. She had not touched the oranges. Antonio had at first been offended that she did not like his gift, since she had made such a display of taking the old woman's oranges weeks before, but he quickly apologized and shared the fruit with Ana while Valentina played a few songs on her guitar.

Ana for her part was even more starry-eyed than before. "Isn't he the nicest man you've ever met?" she asked as they cleaned up the remains of the picnic.

"He's all right, I suppose." Valentina did not like the way he kept staring at her, as if he were trying to see inside her very soul. It made her feel uncomfortable and exposed, something she had never felt in the presence of anyone else, even Dimitri.

"I can't believe he wants us to meet him tomorrow again for

lunch!" Ana placed their used mugs on a nearby bench and bent to pick up the empty milk can. "Do you think he likes me?"

"Of course I do. But I think you'd better get home. Your mother will be looking for you, and I don't want to have to explain to mine what a strange man was doing in our yard," Valentina said.

"I suppose I should get home. *Mother* will be looking for me." She had to force the word *mother* past her lips. Her mother had been anything but a parent to her, despite the nice clothes and money they had. "I'll see you tomorrow," she added. Her earlier brightness was gone. The sorrowful Ana that the villagers mocked had returned.

"Until tomorrow, Ana. Think good thoughts! You'll have your soldier in no time." *I hope,* she added silently.

* * *

The next afternoon was a repeat of the day before. Valentina nudged Antonio in Ana's direction often, even leaving them alone for long stretches while she played with Jorge, the family pig she had brought along. It was an odd choice for a companion, but she hoped her tomboyish nature would deter Antonio's affections, and he would pay more attention to Ana. In a way, her plan seemed to work. While she ran around with Jorge and kept herself occupied, Antonio and Ana talked for quite a while, and he appeared to be more interested in her than the day before. But as they returned home after lunch ended, Valentina could see that Ana was upset. "What's troubling you?" she asked.

"Antonio talked to me all afternoon. But do you know what he talked about? He talked about you. Valentina this and Valentina that! I felt like I was being interrogated by the police! He never asked a single question about me." Ana burst into tears and buried her face in her hands.

Valentina was momentarily speechless. She searched for the right words to make her friend feel better, but nothing seemed to be appropriate. Finally, she simply told the truth. "I don't care for him. But you do, and eventually he'll realize that I am not interested in him. Then you'll have your chance. I've done nothing to encourage him and you know that, Ana."

"Do you really think so?" Ana sniffed. She wiped her eyes with the back of her hand and tried to smile. "It sounds like I would be second choice."

"No! Don't say that! How can you be second choice if I never chose him to begin with? You should be first!" She hoped she sounded convincing. The truth was that she doubted Antonio knew Ana was alive, and it angered her that he could be so callous. But she put on a strong front for Ana's sake. He could think what he wanted. She just wasn't interested in him, not when her heart was set on Dimitri. "Of course you'd be first," she repeated.

"I hope you're right, Valentina," Ana replied, her tears now gone. "I do like him very much."

* * *

Valentina sat in the little window by the front door, strumming a few random chords. Life in *Arrifes* was difficult, she conceded, and it was made more so by the fact that most of the village was very poor.

She kept thinking back to Ana and the soldier, Antonio Fero. Her conscience was busy nagging at her that he was up to no good, and that Ana would only end up being hurt. Her friend wanted so much to meet a good man and move on with her life. The villagers had never been kind to Ana's family, though the men in the village availed themselves of her mother often.

Valentina cringed at the thought. She was not a complete innocent in the ways between a man and a woman. She knew what Ana's mother did for a living, and while the thought made her sick to her stomach, Valentina couldn't help but feel sorry for them. Money was hard to come by when farming and fishing were the only options for the men here. What few managed to escape the poverty and seek better lives in America or in other places like Brazil and Argentina often never returned for their families. It was a lesson learned for Valentina's own family, she thought sadly.

She spied Dimitri walking down her street with several of his friends, and ducked from view. She watched through a crack in the curtain as he paused and glanced at the window, as if he'd known she was watching him. He smiled, shook his head, and resumed walking with his friends towards the center of the village. Valentina let out a sigh of relief when she was sure he was out of sight. She didn't want him thinking that she was watching him. It would only go to his arrogant head. But she smiled in spite of herself. He'd known she was there, and for some reason, that meant more than anything. It took the sting out of her earlier thoughts. Despite his wealth, Dimitri thought nothing of walking down her street and stopping at her window. She suspected she placed more emphasis on their differences than he did, but she had to remain sensible. She would never be good enough for Dimitri Maciel, regardless of how either of them might feel.

That last thought brought tears to her eyes, the truth of it undeniable. Suddenly Valentina was too tired to play anymore, and she quietly readied for bed.

Chapter 3

The park was overflowing with people when Dimitri arrived with several of his friends. Mass had run longer than usual, and by the time the priest offered the final blessing and sent everyone on their way, Dimitri was dying for a cigarette and some fresh air. He strolled along the grounds, searching out Valentina. His friends ran off to flirt with a group of girls that had just arrived. He was beginning to think that Valentina might not be performing that day after all when he heard someone tuning a guitar. Following the sound of the random chords, he came upon a little clearing where Valentina, Ana, Valentina's mother and sister, and several other village women sat. The men stood a respectable distance away, including his father. Ana's mother waited on the fringe of the group, her actions nervous and uncomfortable. A few women, his mother among them, shot her dirty looks every now and then. He grinned when he caught Valentina staring at him. She looked surprised for a moment, then stuck her nose in the air and pretended to look somewhere else. He dropped himself down into the grass and listened as she prepared to sing.

Valentina scanned the crowd casually, as if to see who might be there. She certainly didn't want Dimitri to know she had been looking for *him*. He'd caught her staring once. He wouldn't catch her again. She would play his game and remain as aloof as he did.

She strummed a few chords, adjusting the tension on the strings until they sounded just right. She hummed to the soft sound of her guitar until the sound was perfect. Today she would play and sing until the sun went down.

There was always someone in the crowd with a harmonica in his pocket who would try to follow all of the tunes. Valentina smiled at Mr. Almeida, the 90-year-old "grandfather" of the village who came regularly to the concerts in the park. He would sit across from her, tap his foot in time to the music, and as soon as he had a steady rhythm going, he would join in with his harmonica. Soon the park was filled with the melodies of a dozen instruments as the crowd got into the spirit of the afternoon.

Dimitri closed his eyes as Valentina's sweet, seductive voice washed over him. He'd put off declaring his feelings for her far too long. For years he'd seen her only as the girl he'd grown up with. Somewhere along the way he missed how she'd blossomed into a beautiful, desirable woman. Of course, he'd always thought her pretty. But his reaction to the soldier's inquiries about her the other day made him realize just what she meant to him. The soldier was obviously smitten, and Dimitri would not let anyone come in and steal what belonged to him. He had to speak with her. Tonight, he decided as Valentina continued to fill the air with music.

He glanced around him and saw that the crowd had thickened. He also noticed his rival, the curious soldier, approaching the group. Dimitri took his measure of the man, noting that he walked with a certain arrogance that Valentina would definitely find fault with. He also wore his uniform to see her, even though it was Sunday and he should have been wearing regular clothes. Obviously he needed to show his importance, Dimitri decided. The thought made his stomach turn.

The hours flew as Valentina played. She sang of love, and

Dimitri pretended that she sang of him: "*O meu amor é um cravo/ dequeles que o craveiro deu/ ninguem se gava de ter um cravinho como o meu.*" The buses had arrived with people from nearby villages, and they joined in her songs and broke out in their customary folk dancing. It was almost dark by the time the crowd broke up and everyone went off in search of supper and a good night's sleep. Dimitri knew Valentina would not be headed home just yet. Tonight she would head out to the old woman's orchard and steal a couple of oranges before she went to bed. And this time he would follow her, and tell her how he really felt.

Valentina swung her guitar over her shoulder and shook hands with one of her friends, who complemented her playing before leaving with the rest of her family for the night. She said good night to Ana and her mother, and was about to leave when Antonio stepped in front of her, blocking her exit. "*Boa noite*," he smiled, "can we talk for a bit?" She looked behind her and saw Ana watching them closely. She grinned at her friend, and then turned back to Antonio. "Sure," she said. "I have a few minutes." She also spotted Dimitri watching her very closely. *Let him watch,* she thought as Antonio sat down on a nearby bench and motioned for her to do the same. She placed the guitar on the ground next to her and folded her hands in her lap. "What can I do for you?"

"It's about us," he began, but Valentina raised a hand and cut him off.

"There is no 'us' Antonio. I think I've been pretty clear in how I feel about you. Ana, on the other hand, really cares about you. I think you two would make a fine pair, and you should pursue a relationship with her."

"But I don't want Ana," he protested. "I like you. Ana is plain, boring and we have nothing in common."

"You are despicable! How dare you talk about my friend like

that!" Valentina stood up and grabbed her guitar. "Don't you ever come around me again, Antonio! Do you hear me?" She left before he had a chance to say anything else.

* * *

The night was cool and a welcome relief after the sticky heat of the day. It felt good to stretch and walk after sitting cramped on a stone bench for hours, playing until her fingers were numb and her throat was sore. But she loved the feeling of the crowd at her command, lived for the applause and the admiration that came when a song was played particularly well or a note was sung perfectly. The crowds would even brave the sun as they inched out of the shade to hear her sing. It was an intoxicating sensation, and Valentina felt so alive and free during those few, brief hours. And now she would celebrate her success with a few pilfered oranges from the old woman's orchard. Sour Face went to bed early on Sundays. She never went to the concerts because she thought Valentina's playing was inspired by the devil.

Valentina removed her clogs this time before descending the hill. She easily found her way through the other shrubs in the orchard before coming upon the orange trees. She inhaled their sweet fragrance, laughing as she wondered what the old lady would do if she knew she was being stolen from again.

She was debating which oranges to take when she was startled by a noise behind her. Valentina thought the old woman might have discovered her after all, but her fear turned to annoyance as she saw Dimitri emerge from the trees. "You scared me half to death!" she scolded. "What are you doing, following me here?"

"I need to talk to you." Dimitri had rehearsed his speech all the way to the orchard. Now, standing so close to her, he couldn't think straight. Surprised by his reaction, he turned away and pretended interest in the orange trees. "You're right, these oranges are better than mine."

"That's a lie and you know it." Valentina leaned her guitar against one of the trees and slipped her clogs back on. "Did you come here to see if I'll make a fool of myself and get caught again?"

"No Valentina, no one could ever make a fool of you." Dimitri stepped forward and lightly ran a finger down her cheek. "You're much too smart for that."

Valentina's eyes rounded in shock. Guessing his intent, she placed her hand against his chest to push him away but she didn't try to hold him back. She watched, transfixed, as he slid his hand around to the back of her neck and nudged her closer until they were only a few inches apart. "What are you doing?" she asked in a near whisper.

Dimitri smiled and replied, "This." He cupped her chin in his hand and slowly brushed his lips against hers.

Valentina broke away from him, her body trembling with an odd mixture of need and anger. "Just who do you think you are? You followed me here tonight so you could prove just how arrogant you really are! You know there can't be anything between us!"

Dimitri glared at her, his own fury obvious. "I don't need to prove anything to you or anyone else! I know what you think of me, Valentina Marques. You think I'm a lazy, good for nothing freeloader who doesn't want to work and thinks the world owes him something. You've made it clear more than once how you feel about me. But let me tell you something! You are the most aggravating, infuriating, stuck up little girl I have ever had the misfortune to fall in love with!"

Valentina's ears must have failed her. "What did you just say?" she asked. He leaned in closer to her and quietly said, "I said I love you."

Valentina could not seem to find her voice. She'd always hoped he might notice her, but love? How could he love her? They were so different. How could it ever work?

"Usually when someone says they love you, some kind of response is welcome." Dimitri's expression softened as he noted her confusion. "I'm sorry. I shouldn't have upset you like that. Forget I said anything at all."

"Forget you just said you loved me? Are you insane? I need a minute to think about this!" Valentina sat down on the ground, her mind a jumble of thoughts. Dimitri loved her. Every dream and wish she'd ever had rested on what she would say next. Her rich, successful man might very well be standing right in front of her. Did she want to take the chance? "I'm very confused right now," she finally admitted.

"I know." Dimitri sat down beside her and leaned against a tree. Valentina inched closer so they could sit side by side. She laid her head on his shoulder and sighed.

"How could it work between us? Our wholes lives have been filled with people telling us we come from two different worlds. What would they say now?"

"Well, it doesn't sound like you're totally opposed to the idea of loving me back. You haven't run screaming yet. Why can't we just try this? Who is to stop us if we really love each other? And we really do, don't we?" Dimitri teased her.

The silence between them grew long. Valentina looked into his eyes, such deep blue eyes that held the answer she needed to speak. "Yes, we really do," she answered as she reached up and gently caressed his cheek.

Dimitri chuckled as he kissed her again. "What is so funny?" Valentina demanded.

"I'm just remembering how much we used to fight as children. Now look at us."

"I guess you're right. We've come a long way since then, haven't we?" Valentina stood up and gazed up at the night sky. The stars seemed to twinkle in agreement on this new relationship. She felt Dimitri's arms wrap around her as he too stood and looked up into the sky. "I'd say the heavens are on our side. And yes, we have come a long way from the days of pulling your hair and calling you names."

"You were really a pain then. Not that much has changed." She shrieked as Dimitri swung her up into his arms and spun her around. "Put me down!"

"Tell me you love me first!" He suddenly tripped on a rock and the two went crashing to the ground. "Are you hurt?" he asked as he looked her over for injuries.

Valentina stared past him to the trees above them. "No, I'm fine," she replied. "Look above you."

Dimitri stretched out next to her and glanced upward. Above them, the orange trees had grown together in an odd arc shape, reminding him of a rainbow. "It's like a rainbow," he said aloud. "Do you remember what rainbows represent?" he asked her as he turned to look at her.

Valentina studied the trees. "Promises and covenants and things like that," she said.

"They mean making vows, just like the one I'm making to you tonight." Dimitri sat up, and then helped Valentina do the same. "I vow to love you always, Valentina Marques. The rainbow represents a promise, so I want to promise you under the rainbow that I will love you as long as I live." He kissed her hand and smiled. "Now it's your turn."

"Hold on a second." Valentina reached over for her guitar and began to play. Tears welled up in her eyes as she sang Dimitri a love song she'd written just for him, the words expressing how she felt far better than anything she thought she could come up with. "I love you too," she whispered as she finished the song. She noticed there were tears in his eyes too.

"It's getting late," Dimitri said after a few minutes of comfortable silence. He held Valentina in his arms and watched the trees sway gently in the night air. "We should get back."

"Yes we should." But Valentina never wanted to leave. This moment in time was perfect, as close to paradise as she could ever hope for. "Just a few more minutes," she said as she turned to face him.

"Just a few more," Dimitri agreed as he lowered his mouth to hers. This time his kiss was hungry, insistent. Valentina moaned softly as she felt her world unravel with the touch of his tongue on hers. This was all so new to her; it almost seemed unreal. Slowly she explored the magic of his lips, her timid kisses trying to keep pace with his demanding ones. Dimitri lowered her to the ground, his mouth tracing a path of kisses from her brow to her shoulder. "I've dreamed of this for so long, Valentina. Tell me this is what you want too."

She thought of her family, of the fury they would feel if they knew what she was doing at that moment. But none of that really mattered as Dimitri ran his fingers through her hair and continued to kiss her. She let out a sigh of contentment as he carefully slipped her dress off one shoulder and placed his lips there. "I want this too, Dimitri, so much," she whispered as she gazed into his piercing eyes. She took in his proud, strong features, the soft blond hair that made him stand out from most of the other villagers, and the way his hands felt as they touched her. For so long she had dreamed of being his, of giving herself to him completely. She thought of all the horror stories of the village women who frowned and said they almost died of shame, but dear God, she did not feel guilty and never imagined she would enjoy his touch so much.

Dimitri inhaled Valentina's sweet fragrance, his senses lost to the feel of her in his arms. He ran his lips over her hair and lightly placed a kiss on her forehead. "Let me love you," he urged quietly.

Her heart felt as though it would explode. She took a deep breath and whispered once more, "I am so confused." Their kisses became more demanding; she had to remember to breathe as he kissed her hungrily. Valentina, consumed by her own passion, gave herself to him completely.

In a gruff voice filled with emotion, Dimitri spoke his thoughts. "Valentina, you have completed me."

Valentina was nearly overwhelmed by the strength she felt in his muscular form. His heat was making her hot, and she knew she was losing control as she surrendered to the new feelings erupting inside her. She didn't understand her need to touch and caress him. She sighed and their kisses became wild and ravenous. Her heart pounded furiously. She sucked in a breath and wrapped her arms around his neck, and then kissed him with all the passion and longing that he instilled in her.

It was all the encouragement Dimitri needed. They made love beneath the trees, the dark, tranquil night a witness to their pledge of love and devotion forever sealed. Valentina had never felt more afraid or more alive in her life. At last she had the man of her dreams safely in her arms, and he loved her more than anything on earth. Though these feelings and sensations were so new to one so young and inexperienced, she knew the rightness of their joining. On that hot summer night they both lost their innocence, their first taste of love shared only with each other. They spent hours afterward talking about their dreams, his of being a famous doctor and hers of being the greatest singer that ever lived. Dimitri held Valentina close to him, loving her teasing smile, and Valentina reveled in the way he studied her face with such intensity.

The pure joy of this first night together later lulled her into a light but peaceful sleep as the first rays of the sun edged over the hills and brushed the orchard with the soft light of morning. She closed her eyes to the sweet songs of the morning birds, and Dimitri's strong arms wrapped around her.

Chapter 4

Valentina strolled home, a wide grin on her lips. She looked a little disheveled, but she didn't care. She passed Ana on the way to her house and greeted her warmly. "You look different," Ana noted. She considered her friend's appearance a moment, and then a deep crimson flushed her cheeks. "Good Lord, you didn't."

"What?" Valentina asked. She continued walking towards her house, then opened the small gate to the backyard and stepped inside. Ana raced to keep up with her. She had been so dumbstruck that she hadn't even noticed Valentina was no longer standing next to her.

"You and Dimitri? Are you crazy? Your mother will know! Remember the story of the eyes? The old women say that your eyes stop shining the first time you give yourself to a man. But your eyes are shining even more now than they usually do. Oh my God!" Ana sat down heavily on a nearby bench and fanned herself with her hand. "What was it like?" she asked after several minutes.

"It was wonderful! I'm in love, Ana, and I feel like I'm floating in the clouds!" Valentina spun around, laughing as Ana joined her and they danced together in the yard. They collapsed onto the grass and giggled like little girls.

"I've never been so happy, Ana," Valentina confided. "I feel like I'm finally complete."

"I'm so happy for you," Ana replied, her expression wistful. "Maybe it will be my turn soon."

"Maybe very soon," Valentina added hopefully.

They were so caught up in their reverie that neither of them noticed Antonio walk by the gate, his expression murderous. He had heard their conversation. The picnic basket he held in one hand slipped to the ground, forgotten. Valentina had given herself to that good for nothing Dimitri Maciel. Antonio had seen the way he looked at her with such possessiveness that it made his stomach turn to think about it. Well, he reasoned, if she could give herself to such a worthless excuse for a man, then she would most certainly give herself to him. He would not let that thieving bastard have what rightfully belonged to him. He had courted her. He had spent what little money he had on food and presents for Valentina and that annoying friend of hers who fawned over him whenever they were together. How dare she not appreciate all the trouble he'd gone to for her! He would teach Valentina not to cast him aside like just another love struck admirer. He turned and hurried away from the gate, a plan beginning to form in his mind.

* * *

Valentina and Ana talked for hours. She gave little away to her curious friend, only saying that when her turn came it would be absolutely wonderful. "I still can't believe it," Valentina admitted.

"But what will you do now?" Ana asked. "His family doesn't approve of you."

"Dimitri says it doesn't matter what they think. He loves me and I love him, and that's all that matters now. The rest will take care of itself."

"I hope you're right," Ana replied. She then cautioned, "Just be careful. Dimitri's mother is known for her awful temper. She might not be too pleased with you as her future daughter-in-law."

"Not to worry, Ana. I know she'll come around once she sees how in love we are. Why would she want to deny her only son his happiness? It will all turn out exactly as it should. And as for you," Valentina grinned mischievously, "soon Antonio will be declaring his love for you, and you will live happily together as well." Valentina reached to open the gate, but something blocked it from swinging open fully. She looked down and noticed a basket of food on the ground, a half dozen ripe, juicy oranges sitting on top. Fear snaked through her, and for a moment she seemed incapable of movement. Antonio had been here, she realized as terror settled low in her belly.

Ana broke the spell by squealing with delight at the find. "Look! Antonio must have brought these by as a surprise. Aren't they delicious looking?" She reached for the basket and swung it onto one arm. "Should we have some?"

"No!" Valentina said a little too quickly. "What I mean is I'm not hungry. Take the basket home and share those with your mother." Valentina stepped back into the yard and slammed the gate closed, placing a barrier between her and the frightening omen. She could not shake the feeling that there was something ominous about the sudden appearance of the basket. Had he heard their earlier conversation? Did Antonio know about what she and Dimitri did the night before? She told herself it didn't matter what he thought because she wasn't interested in him, but he scared her a little with his intensity and determination to woo her. She had every right to refuse his advances. After all, she didn't love him and she had made herself clear. What more could she do besides flat out tell him to leave her alone?

Valentina shook off her worries and said good-bye to Ana.

Nothing really mattered now except Dimitri, and soon they would be together forever. Her worries were for nothing, she tried to reassure herself.

* * *

Dimitri sat on his porch, leaned his chair back against the wall and watched the villagers walking in the street. His mind kept replaying the night before, and he couldn't stop smiling. He remembered the feel of Valentina's hair through his fingers, hair so soft and shimmery that it reminded him of spun gold. Her mesmerizing moss green eyes widened in surprise as he whispered to her all the things he'd been dying to say ever since he realized just how much he loved her. And his name on her lips was the seal on the promises they made to each other. Their first time together was branded into his memory forever. And he couldn't be happier.

He knew there were obstacles in their way. His family would never agree to his choice of Valentina as a wife. But what did it matter? He wanted to be with her, and she with him. They didn't need anyone or anything else. He smiled to himself, his thoughts again drifting to the night before. Nothing would stand in their way, or ruin their chance at happiness.

* * *

Valentina hung the bed linens on the line in the yard, her mind on anything else except her chores. Dimitri promised to sneak over tonight, since her mother was off helping her friends with the preparation of the harvesting of the corn. It had been more than two weeks since their first wonderful night together. They had seen much of each other since, but Valentina had avoided being alone with him again. Avoidance was best because she knew she wouldn't be able to resist him, and their relationship, for now, had to be kept secret. But tonight would be different. Tonight they could be together without the watchful eyes of the village on them, or the fear of getting caught by either one of their families. He had asked her to leave the gate open, as well as the back door to the kitchen. She would be waiting for him in the front room, and she would wear the dress she had made in his favorite color, a soft, pale green that set off her eyes. Valentina had even cooked a special meal for tonight, and couldn't wait for sunset so they could be together. She finished hanging the sheets and picked up her laundry basket. Taking one last look to make sure the gate was unlocked, she went inside the house.

As she put away the basket and straightened up around the house, Valentina reminisced over their encounter in the orchard. She missed the feel of his strong, protective arms around her, the way he held her close and whispered how much he loved her. Tonight they would have the chance to recreate the magic they'd shared beneath the orange trees.

Valentina went to her bedroom and changed into her new dress. The soft, light fabric skimmed over her and she inhaled the sweet, delicate scent of the lavender perfume Ana had let her borrow. Her co-conspirator had even let her use a pair of pretty shoes to match the dress, but Valentina stood barefoot in her room, the freedom of the night that lay ahead making her a little rebellious. She hoped Dimitri would get there soon. They had a lot of time to make up for.

* * *

"I need to go into the village. You need to stay here and help your mother because she's not feeling well."

"But Father, I have to go out tonight," Dimitri replied.

"You heard what I said, Dimitri. Stay with her and make sure she's comfortable." Dr. Maciel grabbed his bag and hat. "I'll be at the Arruda's. Mrs. Arruda is delivering tonight. I expect you here when I get home." He strode to the front door and left.

There was no use arguing with the old man when he was in a foul mood, Dimitri realized. He stared out the window and watched as the sun sank lower on the horizon, his thoughts on Valentina. What would she think when he didn't show up tonight? Would she think he had deserted her? Dimitri tried not to give light to such negative thoughts as he stalked to the kitchen to heat water for his mother's tea. Going against his father would get him into more trouble than he could afford, especially since he had yet to tell them of Valentina. He knew she would understand, he determined. He would explain everything to Valentina tomorrow and apologize for not coming. And he knew exactly how to make it up to her, he smiled.

* * *

Valentina picked up her guitar and looked at the song she had composed. She started to sing, "Dimitri, nome tào doçe, lindo no chamar/tu vás ser o meu esposo, se o Deus do çeu destinar." As she finished playing she heard the back door creak open. "He's here," she whispered into the empty room. She straightened her skirt, pinched her cheeks for color and sat up straighter on her bench. Any second now he would walk through the door and into her arms. "I'm so happy to see…" Her voice trailed off as she watched Antonio stagger into the room. He reeked of alcohol and stumbled as he came towards her.

"Not expecting me, Valentina? Were you hoping it was your lover boy?" His words were slurred, but Valentina understood enough to realize that he knew about her and Dimitri.

"How dare you! You have no right to be here! Go home and sleep off whatever you drank tonight. What would Ana think if she saw you like this?" She hoped she sounded braver than she felt. But with every step closer that he took, Valentina became more afraid. And where was Dimitri?

"I don't give a damn for your friend Ana! I would never waste my time bedding that horse-faced excuse for a woman! She's definitely nothing like her mother." Antonio advanced further into the room, pulling off his jacket. "She was very nice. But then again, I wasn't too bad myself."

"You're despicable! Get out of my house!" Valentina stood abruptly and put some distance between them. "You're a pig and not worthy enough to have someone like Ana care for you!"

"That's the problem Valentina. I don't want Ana to care for me. I want you to care for me, just like you cared for that useless Dimitri Maciel. I know all about the two of you. I could have given you so much more than he ever could. But that wasn't good enough for a *puta* like you. That doesn't matter any more though. I expect the same treatment you gave him."

For a brief moment they stood in silence. Valentina's voice failed her as she watched Antonio study her, his glaring eyes increasing her unease. Pressure settled in her chest like a large stone had lodged itself within her, and Valentina had to remind herself to breathe. The incessant buzzing of a stray fly in the house brought her back to the present, and Valentina knew that she had to run from Antonio before it was too late.

Antonio also seemed to break out of his reverie. He blocked Valentina's escape, dodging around her in a slow, twisted dance, but he did not touch her. However, she saw his intent inscribed in his dark, alcohol-glazed eyes. She shook, panicked, as she tried to plead with him. "Please, Antonio, don't disgrace me! I'm asking you to be sensible. No decent man will want me once he knows of this, not even Dimitri."

Antonio laughed, a hateful sound that made it difficult for Valentina to get control of her emotions. "You are so beautiful, Valentina," he said, a wicked grin spreading across his face. "People treat you like a child, but one look at you and anyone can see you're all woman." He advanced towards her, his hands clenching in anticipation.

Valentina shook with rage. "I won't let you touch me! Let me pass or I'll scream!"

"What do you think they'll say, Valentina?" he sneered as he inched closer. She could smell his foul breath now, see the dark glint of lust in his half closed eyes. "Why did you let me in? Everyone knows you've been flaunting yourself in front of me, teasing me and tempting me just like the devil himself."

Valentina stumbled back and almost fell. She caught herself on a bench and shoved it at him. "You're a drunk! You walk like a drunk and talk like a drunk! How dare you come into my house and give the impression that I've tempted you! What do you think the villagers would say? Get out!" she screamed.

Things were happening too fast. In a last effort to get Antonio to see reason, Valentina begged, "Please think of what you're doing, Antonio! If you force this cruel and immoral act on me, you'll be damned to hell!"

"Don't you understand?" he shouted. "I love you!"

"Love me?" Valentina's voice was harsh as she retorted, "You don't love me! The only thing you are showing me is my destruction. No man will want me! You are heartless!"

Tears coursed down her face as she saw Antonio tremble, confusion halting him for a moment. But the wine in his blood was stronger, and she could see the powers of evil working within him. Desperation grew with each step he took towards her. Valentina fought him off with every fiber of her being, but she was no match for his superior strength. With great anguish she punched, clawed and squirmed in an attempt to free herself from his grip.

Antonio laughed again, but his expression was furious as he trapped her arm in his grip and twisted it. He let out a loud, frustrated sigh as he yanked her to the floor and tore at her clothes, covering her body with his. He moaned and grunted like a wild animal in heat. Valentina heard herself speak as though she were far away. "I have just lost my Dimitri! How will I survive this shameful secret?" The last lucid thought she had was her humiliation and betrayal to Dimitri. As that fact registered in Valentina's mind she felt as if she were falling, dropping into a deep abyss. Her world went black.

Chapter 5

Antonio shook his head to clear it, but all he managed to do was make the pounding worse. He had no idea how he came to be outside the local tavern, or even what time it was. But he did know that he had to hide, and quickly. The army base was in *Ponta Delgada*, which bordered *Arrifes*. The solders would often frequent *Arrifes* for many services, such as the washing of their clothes or the hiring of a seamstress, and it was normal for them to go in and out of the village with no problem. Many, however, took advantage of the benefits in the nearby village and would take other, less moral liberties.

Antonio had heard the rumors about *Arrifes*, how if a man harmed any of the village women or did anything inappropriate, he would be hurt in some way, and in some cases a man's body simply disappeared. One soldier he knew had lived to tell about it. He'd been following a girl around, thinking she was 16 years old and old enough to return his attentions. When he learned her real age, however, he continued to pursue her. One night after a feast, just as he was leaving, he was pulled into a cornfield and all he could see in the dark was the shine of the knife blade coming at him. They had cut him up pretty badly, and his face had taken so many punches that his eyes were swollen shut. It had taken days for him to be able to see. He'd also suffered multiple stab wounds, but they hadn't wanted to kill him. His battered body was found outside the protective base wall. They had wanted to send a message.

Although Antonio was drunk, his senses told him danger lurked close by. His fear mechanism sounded the alert buzzer in his head. He started to run. He knew he ran the risk of going in circles, and he felt like he was chasing the darkness, stumbling and falling over a stone wall and landing in a cornfield. He looked around but saw nothing in the dark, and he again remembered the story. Even now they were most likely looking for him. Antonio collapsed in terror, breathing heavily. *They'll kill me or beat me until I'm unconscious or dead,* he thought with growing panic. Every pinprick he felt as he ran through the field became a stabbing of the knife.

In the dark of night, with only the moonlight dimly lighting his path, Antonio looked frantically around, trying to concentrate on which way led out of the cornfield. He didn't want to face the threat of a hostile presence. He was so scared he envisioned the plunges of the knife into his pulsating body. He was feeling the unbearable pain that could mean the end of his survival. In the shroud of darkness panic stole his breath away. Would he survive an assault? He was drowning in his own fear. Just as he was about to lift his head for a much needed gasp of air, he heard something heavy crash down beside him. Antonio lay paralyzed in fear, terrified of being found. His heart was pounding and his face lay pressed against the cold stone wall. He was frozen in place, afraid to breath. He listened to nearby whispers, and from what he could tell he guessed there were two of them. They must be searching for him. If he was found, he knew he would not leave the village alive.

As he strained to listen, the whispers were becoming faint. Antonio knew he had to make his move now. His only escape would be to roll back over the stone wall. With that thought he instinctively lowered his head over the wall, and with a thud the rest of his body followed. For the first time in Antonio's life he appreciated the size of his form. He was small enough to inch his way the whole length of the wall that led back to the tavern. Antonio knew he was coming to the end of the wall that had shielded him. The dim lights of the tavern came into focus. He hesitated to stand, but he had to in order not to look suspicious. Slowly he rose, looked around, and put his hands in his pockets. He tried to walk casually and he nodded "*Boa noite*" to the two remaining men finishing their card game. He was so close to the gates leading out of *Arrifes.* As soon as he passed through them, he looked back once, and then picked up his pace, nearly running when he saw nothing.

About a block away Antonio sat in the doorway of a building and caught his breath. He knew he had to come up with a plan. Tonight he escaped. Next time he might not be so lucky. Tonight he searched out Valentina to satisfy the urgent demands of his own body, and in the process left her with feelings of hate, failure, and tears of sorrow. He hadn't cared what he'd done to her. Through the dull thudding in his brain he still hadn't fathomed the full impact of his actions.

Antonio tried to stand on shaky legs, his resolve gathering strength. He would not let his fear of some hoodlums from *Arrifes* keep him from satisfying his needs and desires. He would outsmart them again, and he would have Valentina as many times as it suited him.

With that decision firmly planted in his mind, Antonio staggered back to the base, his mind on a warm bed and a good night's sleep.

Chapter 6

Sour Face, or Mrs. DaSilva as she was more formally known, slowly shuffled her way home, a wide grin splitting her ancient, cracked lips to show the oversized and rotting teeth within. She carefully hugged her bundle of cheese and biscuits to her chest, her reward for the information she'd passed on to Mrs. Maciel earlier that morning.

She recalled the night about two weeks ago when she'd been awakened by laughter coming from the orchard. She had picked her way through the orange trees and spied Mrs. Maciel's son Dimitri on top of that irritating little thief Valentina Marques. She'd watched, transfixed by some jealous curiosity as they had made love into the night. Her smile faded as she considered the impoverished Valentina in the arms of the rich and handsome doctor's son. It was not fair that those two should find happiness with each other while she had no one to share her life with.

She'd kept her discovery a secret, waiting for the right moment to approach Mrs. Maciel. There had to be something in it for her before she would come forward. And then the moment had come. She'd seen Antonio Fero, the besotted drunk who followed Valentina around like a lovesick dog, stagger down her street last night. He'd mumbled something about Valentina and from what she could make out, she reasoned they had spent the night together. She'd gone straight to Mrs. Maciel first thing this morning, hoping she might be compensated for what she had to say. And Mrs. Maciel had found her information most useful.

"You saw what?" Mrs. Maciel had asked, incredulous.

"Valentina Marques was having her way with your son," she'd replied.

"That *puta*! How dare she seduce my son! I will not stand for this!" Mrs. Maciel ordered one of her maids to bring some food for the old woman. "For your trouble, Mrs. DaSilva," she'd said as she presented the small bundle.

She forced a smile. *Mrs.* DaSilva indeed. It was a title of respect, not because Mr. DaSilva existed somewhere. "Thank you, Mrs. Maciel."

"Thank you for bringing this to my attention. I will speak to her immediately," Mrs. Maciel seethed.

"I'll tell her you wish to speak with her," she offered as she backed towards the door. "No trouble at all."

Now you'll get what you deserve for stealing from me, the old woman grinned, thinking of poor, foolish Valentina up against the imposing Mrs. Maciel. The stupid girl was done for.

* * *

Valentina squinted her eyes against the bright sunlight streaming through her window. She rolled over and winced when she landed on her bruised ribs. Remembering how she'd gotten the bruises brought tears to her eyes. The night before burned in her mind and Valentina felt the urge to vomit. She dragged herself from bed and managed to get outside to the backyard before the nausea overtook her. She chanced a look at the street beyond the gate. The villagers were already up and beginning their day. Did any of them know? Did they know Antonio had come into her house last night and raped her? The thought again made her sick, and she was glad her mother had already left for the day. Valentina had cleaned up the mess in the front room before she'd gotten home in the early hours of the morning, and thankfully her mother had not awakened her before she left this morning. Valentina reached for the water bucket and filled it at the pump, her mind on Dimitri. Where had he been the night before? Why hadn't he come?

As she carried the bucket back to the house, Sour Face passed by her gate. "Good morning Valentina," she sneered.

Valentina looked up and saw the old woman smiling. "I heard your concert last week was very good," she said, and Valentina felt a chill race down her spine.

"Thank you," she replied uneasily, but the old woman was already walking away.

She shook off the odd encounter and went inside. Valentina poured the water into the cauldron hanging over the fireplace and waited for the water to heat up. She then scrubbed herself from head to toe, the memory of Antonio's hands on her making her scrub until she bled. Her beautiful new dress had been burned in the fireplace along with the sheet she'd used to clean herself with after he'd staggered out of the house and collapsed in the yard. She'd had to drag him to the end of the street, her mind in constant fear that someone would catch her out at that hour. She dumped him in front of the village tavern and raced home, then bolted the doors and watched the house fearfully until she fell into a troubled sleep, a kitchen knife clutched in one hand.

How would she now face Dimitri? Would he be able to tell that Antonio had violated her? Would he even believe her? It was no secret that Antonio was smitten with her. Would Dimitri ever look at her the same way again?

She had been ready to say so much to Dimitri the night before. Valentina thought it was time their families knew how they felt about each other, even though they knew no one would approve. She also had something else to share with him. She was pregnant. Valentina absently placed a hand over her belly. It had only been two weeks, but she was sure. She was going to be a mother. Her mind did not let her consider that Antonio may have somehow hurt the baby the night before. She instead thought of how happy she felt over the new life growing inside of her, and of Dimitri's reaction when she told him. She prayed he would be happy.

Suddenly the house felt very oppressive and Valentina needed air. It wasn't the thought of telling Dimitri what had happened that bothered her. Something else nagged at her subconscious, but she couldn't put her finger on it. She finished washing up and hastily threw on some clothes. Her hair still dripping from her bath, Valentina left the house, careful to avoid any place where Antonio might be at this hour. She headed for the orchard to think and perhaps steal an orange or two.

Valentina was kneeling by a very large orange tree when she felt a presence behind her. She searched the shadows of the trees as she called out, fearful that Antonio had come to find her. Sour Face emerged from the trees, and Valentina knew she was caught. But the old woman did not seem angry that she had been stealing oranges again. She looked rather smug, and again Valentina felt a chill. "You may keep the oranges," the old woman said before Valentina had a chance to speak. "That is not the reason I came upon you. You might as well take three more for tomorrow," she added, indicating the oranges still hanging on the tree. "Leave them wrapped in your apron." She smiled again, exposing her protruding teeth, and suddenly Valentina knew real fear. "Mrs. Maciel wants to talk to you. Go now, she is waiting for you." The old woman walked away, and Valentina could feel the flush of embarrassment staining her cheeks. Mrs. Maciel knew she was here, and that she stole from Sour Face. Valentina dropped her apron and left as fast as she could, wondering why she had been summoned to the grand Maciel house.

Her knock on the front door was answered by the housekeeper. It opened into a very large dining room, where Valentina was told to wait. She walked around the elaborate table, which was covered with very expensive embroidered linens, as well as two tall, silver candelabras that surrounded the centerpiece. It was packed with Rose of Sharon and lush greens, no doubt picked from the house's own gardens. She inhaled the sweet scent that filled the room, wondering if Dimitri was here. Had he told his mother about them? Had she been summoned here in friendship, or something else?

Valentina continued her inspection of the room, her eyes roaming over the mahogany chairs that were nearly as tall as she was. She frowned as she realized the value of those chairs, so much more regal than the two benches she and her mother used in their kitchen. She began to feel very small and out of place. Perhaps this was not meant to be a friendly visit at all, but a way of intimidating her into leaving Dimitri alone.

She ran a hand across the back of one of the chairs. So rich and elegant. What would it be like to sit in such a grand chair each night for supper? A sudden chill interrupted Valentina's thoughts and she turned around as someone entered. Mrs. Maciel made her grand entrance into the room. She was an unattractive woman, her thick build overemphasized by her large breasts that were as high on her body as her tight hair bun, which sat like a diadem upon her head. She took the chair at the head of the table, but did not offer Valentina a seat. *Time to stand up for myself,* Valentina decided as she took a chair to Mrs. Maciel's left. Mrs. Maciel raised an eyebrow but did not comment until Valentina was settled. Her mouth was as tight as a knotted bow as she pointed an accusatory finger at Valentina. "I will make myself very clear.

I do not like you or the free-spirited individual you represent. You are no longer a girl to go and sit in the village square with a guitar and to use your voice and flash more than your ankles to lure my son." She smiled coldly and added, "I also know what goes on in the orchard across the street. Under the cover of the trees, you pick more than oranges."

Valentina's mouth dropped open. How did she know? She then remembered the old woman's strange behavior that morning. Sour Face had sold her out. "Look, Mrs. Maciel…" Valentina began, but the older woman cut her off.

"You are going to have to get past your embarrassment to be able to understand every word that I am going to say to you." Valentina never flinched. She sat as straight as a rod in her chair. Not even a blink of an eye gave away her unease. Mrs. Maciel continued. "Should you trap my son into marrying you by getting pregnant, any bastard child born to you will not be acknowledged. You will tell my son that you are in love with someone else, maybe that soldier who follows you around. Everyone knows he wants to marry you. If you have any true courage you will leave this village and marry him before word gets out that you're not only using your talent to entice men, but also your body." She spoke to Valentina as one did to a servant. The room had become uncomfortably quiet. Valentina felt heat build up in her face that she knew was from mortification. She hoped Mrs. Maciel would not mention it to her again.

She waited for Valentina to get hold of herself. But how could Valentina answer her when she could not find her voice, her head sagging and her knees shaking? For the first time her spirit was broken. Her heartache was like nothing she had ever experienced. Without physically attaching it, Mrs. Maciel had placed a brand upon Valentina's breast. She could barely keep from bursting into tears. She chanced a look at Dimitri's mother.

Somehow Mrs. Maciel's words were muted, and Valentina found herself staring at her. She felt trapped in a fog as she looked at the hard line of Mrs. Maciel's mouth. Her throat ached with her need to shout out, to protect herself from the venom the other woman issued forth.

As if reading Valentina's mind, Mrs. Maciel spat out, "From my son, there will never be a marriage proposal to you, let alone a marriage! I am being very kind to you. Dr. Maciel and I have plans for our son. His primary duty, his only duty, is to go on to medical school in Lisbon. There also awaits his future wife. She has been promised to him since the day she was born. She comes from the same class of people as Dimitri's paternal grandmother. She is actually a distant cousin of Dr. Maciel's. Dimitri will never marry the likes of you. I do not want anything to happen to you should you decide to stay and not go off with the soldier boy." Mrs. Maciel held up a hand before Valentina could interrupt. "Yes, the whole village knows he follows you around like a lovesick little boy. You walk around, a temptress with your hair flowing in the wind. You're no longer a girl, Valentina. Pick up your hair, braid it and secure it with combs so it stays in place. And while you're securing your hair, you should do the same with your breasts. They are as loose as your hair." To emphasize her last point, Mrs. Maciel sat up straighter in her chair. Her restrictive corset did nothing to hide the bulges that were too great to hold in. If she weren't in so much pain, Valentina would have thought it funny.

But Valentina's mood was anything but amused. Her jaw fell again as she contemplated the awful words spilling from Mrs. Maciel's lips. It took a great deal of restraint not to fall to the floor, curl up into a ball and cry. It was true that she and Dimitri did not share the same class. And yes, perhaps she was much more independent than the other girls in the village. She did not have Ana's money to buy fancy corsets to bind her, and her hair was long and loose because she liked it that way. She would not compromise herself for the likes of Mrs. Maciel, or anyone else.

She did not know how long she stared at the older woman, but she was done taking her abuse. She regrouped what dignity she had left, and her green eyes sparkled with an unspoken challenge. Mrs. Maciel visibly cringed as she saw the change in Valentina's composure. Valentina had bitten her tongue long enough—now she was angry. But she forced herself to stay calm before she snapped out, "I am beginning to understand now. This is all my fault, of course, and you are threatening me. Correct?" Valentina did not give her a chance to answer, but continued her tirade. "You want me to leave my family and my friends because you obviously fear the future. But I will make you one promise if I leave my village. And yes, you heard me right. This is *my* village. You, your husband and your son are the outsiders who invaded us under the pretense of healing the sick, but it was all for your personal gain. How kind of your husband to say that if a villager couldn't pay with money, he'd take a fattened pig or a dozen fresh eggs, when he knows very well how little most of these people have. When I leave, and if I ever see Dimitri again, I will tell him everything we have discussed today. I hope and pray that I will never find a way to right the wrong you have done to me today. I do not have a father around. I live with my mother and sister in a small house no bigger than a hut, and I do not have fancy clothes or shoes. My mother and sister cook and clean in fancy houses like this one to put food on the table. It is their agreement that I use my talent to sing, and yes, I do get paid when I sing to entertain. We are poor and we have no money, and we live day to day, but one thing we do have in abundance is love." Valentina finally took a deep breath. She was both relieved and surprised by her own words. Mrs. Maciel would not treat her like some pitiful servant. She would make herself heard before she faced the most painful decision of her life. She braced herself for whatever else Mrs. Maciel might be preparing to throw at her.

Shocked and taken aback by Valentina's bold attitude, Mrs. Maciel was stunned silent. No one would ever have voiced their opinions to her like that, let alone stand up to her. She had to admire the foolish girl's courage. She was, after all, the wife of Dr. Maciel, and everyone knew she was measured by his shadow. She briefly reflected on him and her son before dealing with Valentina. Tall and business savvy, Joaquim Maciel was the ideal husband for her social position. And at twenty-two, Dimitri resembled his father in every way. It was only a matter of time before he followed in his father's footsteps and went off to Lisbon for his medical degree. She would not let this little tramp ruin her only child's chances for fortune and success. She masked her earlier surprise, rose from the table and said, "Now who is threatening whom?" She pushed in her chair and left the room, an obvious dismissal.

Before she stepped through the door, Mrs. Maciel turned around and added, "You know you are way out of your league to lock horns with me. I do not want to see you anywhere near my son. Do you understand me?" She waved a hand towards the other door. "You may leave the same way you came in." She spun around and left.

Valentina carefully rose from her seat, tears dangerously close to falling. *I will not cry in this house,* she thought. She wouldn't give Mrs. Maciel the satisfaction of seeing her crumble inside the grand Maciel home. Valentina walked out of the dining room and opened the front door. The sun momentarily blinded her as she stepped out into the hot afternoon. She passed several villagers on the street but made no eye contact with anyone. She also prayed that she would not see Dimitri today. She couldn't handle looking him in the eye after what his mother had just said to her.

How could someone be so cruel? It was common knowledge that Mrs. Maciel married her husband for his name and his money. Was that all the woman cared about? Did she not feel love for her family? Valentina shook her head. Mrs. Maciel had ice for a heart. She could no more feel love than the sun could light the night sky.

But for all that she was, Mrs. Maciel was right. Dimitri would never marry her. Despite the promises he'd made to her, he could not hurt his family and ruin his chances at a successful career. And if there really was a woman waiting for him in Lisbon…the thought of it made Valentina sick to her stomach. He would fight for her, and they would both lose. And one day he might come to resent how she destroyed his life.

Valentina knew the choice had to lie with her. If Dimitri found out about what Antonio did to her, he would kill that disgusting pig. While Valentina wouldn't mind Antonio's removal from this earth, she knew Dimitri would go to jail and it would all be her fault. Or worse, he might not believe her and think she wanted Antonio, and he would hate her forever. No matter what, she had to end it between them. There was no way that they could win in this. With a heavy heart and the tears finally pouring from her eyes, Valentina walked in her backyard gate and lay down on the soft green grass, her muffled sobs filling the quiet afternoon.

Chapter 7

Valentina did not know how long she lay on the grass, her mind going over everything that had happened in the last few months. It all seemed like a very long nightmare. Life had started to look so perfect, first with her music finally paying off for her family, then with Dimitri's declaration of love for her. But their happiness wasn't destined to last. Antonio had made sure of that. He had compromised Valentina's position in the community and with her family. And now she would have to make the most painful choice of her life. She knew Dimitri could never accept her now. She felt dirty, ashamed that Antonio had touched and used her. Deep down she believed Dimitri would accept her no matter what had happened, but his position and family status would compromise any chance they might have still had. It was time to let him go, she thought miserably. She would have no choice. If she wanted her child to have a father and a life, she would have to let Dimitri go and accept her fate.

She rose from the ground, her body stiff from lying there so long. She went into the house and sat by the fireplace to fight off the sudden chill she felt. Dimitri might very well be disgusted with her if he found out what happened. She could not live with that guilt. How could their love survive any of the arrows that had been sent to pierce their devotion to each other? Mrs. Maciel had been more than clear, and Antonio's betrayal left her no other options. There were a few things she would need to do first, but before she lost her nerve, Valentina would tell Dimitri it was over.

She was feeling very self-conscious about her appearance after the encounter with Dimitri's mother. She walked over to Ana's house and asked her to tell Dimitri to meet her in the orchard later that evening. "But why don't you ask him yourself?" Ana asked. She stared at her friend. Valentina looked terrible, as if she'd been crying for a very long time. Something was very wrong, but Valentina just shook her head.

"I need to go home and get ready. I must look awful." Today would be the last time Dimitri would lay eyes on her, and for that reason, she wanted to look her very best.

"Okay, I'll go." Ana went off in search of Dimitri. Something was brewing, and she did not like it one bit. Why did she have the feeling that something awful was about to happen? Ana shrugged her shoulders and headed to the wealthy side of the village. She would find out soon enough, she supposed.

Valentina returned home and searched through some of her sister's clothes for a more suitable dress than the ones she owned. She borrowed a beautiful red dress with a loose skirt and fitted bodice. She skipped the petticoat so that the dress outlined her curves through the fabric. The high lace collar cupped her face and the long, fitted sleeves felt snug against her arms. The dress was no longer in style, but it accented her hourglass figure perfectly. Valentina swept her hair up onto the top of her head and secured it with combs, and attached a red rose. Her earlier attempts to create a tight bun like Ana's failed miserably, and this new style didn't look like it would hold for very long either. By the time she had gotten halfway to the orchard, the hot and humid weather had caused her hair to come loose, and instead of the elegant twists atop her head, her hair was now a riot of curls cascading down her back. This was why Valentina hated putting her hair up. She'd wanted to look her best for Dimitri because this would be the last image she would leave him with. So far her attempts at a little glamour were not working. Her feet were also starting to hurt from never wearing shoes. She pulled the black, heeled shoes she had borrowed from Ana off her feet and carried them instead. Her feet were burning with discomfort by the time she reached the orchard. "So much for elegance," she grumbled as she made her way through the trees.

She found Dimitri sitting against a large tree trunk. He stood when he heard her whispered voice calling to him. For a moment he froze, statue-like, until his brain reminded him to move his limbs again, and he closed the distance between himself and Valentina. The state of her dishevelment did not disguise her beauty. His heart skipped a beat as he looked her over. Never had he seen someone more beautiful, more grown-up and so much a woman. She too seemed frozen in place. He stared at her, the sheer pleasure of simply taking in her appearance enough for the moment. Her wide eyes called to him, their color as green as the lush trees around them, and involuntarily he reached out for her. Their eyes locked onto each other, and they stood motionless a moment more, until finally the urge to touch her overcame Dimitri's paralysis and he pulled her into his arms. The power of her beauty captivated him, and he reveled in the feel of her.

Valentina closed her eyes and breathed in his scent, her senses reeling and her stomach fluttering with nervous energy. She glanced up at him and said meekly, "There is something I need to tell you." She pulled away from him slightly and took a deep breath. "Today we have to say good-bye."

Dimitri felt as if someone had just punched him. She had to be joking, he tried to convince himself. Of course she was. He felt instantly calmer and said, "I don't believe you," He batted his blue eyes at her, teasing her. "What do you really want to tell me?"

Valentina lowered her head. It was torturous to meet his gaze. The slight breeze had blown her hair across her face, but she made no move to pull it back. She did not want him to see her pain. She struggled for her voice and managed to say, "It is true, Dimitri. I am to be married to a very rich man, and he will take me away from my misery."

"You're talking nonsense Valentina. Why are you saying these awful things to me?" Dimitri stepped forward, but she retreated backwards. She was still afraid to raise her eyes to his, so Dimitri cupped her chin and forced her to look up at him. He tucked her hair behind her ear. "What's wrong?" he asked gently. "Has someone said something to you about us? Did my mother say anything to upset you?"

"No, it's nothing like that," Valentina lied. Tears welled up in her eyes as she studied the man before her. She had never been more aware of his handsome face and strong, powerful body. She wanted to imprint his image in her mind, the soft, golden blonde hair, his broad, steady shoulders, the straight, proud nose, high cheekbones, and the startling blue eyes the color of a noonday sky that now appeared to be in so much turmoil. She had put that pain there, and the thought spilled forth her tears. She tried to wipe them away, but they only came down faster.

Dimitri's face seemed to crumble. His strong, square jaw trembled as he too tried hard to compose himself. He moved toward her again and his white shirt strained against the muscles in his chest and arms. He took Valentina's breath away, and she could not believe she was about to give up this man who meant more than anything else in this world to her. But she had to finish this, and though she could feel her heart shattering in a million pieces, she steadied her shoulders and looked again into his eyes.

Dimitri's emotions were at war within him. His familiar mocking grin was replaced with a sincere but pained expression as he said quietly, "I have been waiting for you to grow up, Valentina."

She frowned, confused. What did he mean? "I don't understand," she replied. She looked down at his chest and tried to disguise her own weakening resolve. Why did this have to be so hard? Dimitri was not going to make this easier either. Valentina sighed in frustration as she contemplated what she would say next. Dimitri looked ready to reply to her question, but she held out her hand, palm up, to stop him. "Wait. Before you answer that, I have to explain."

"But let me tell you," Dimitri tried.

"Hush, please." She gazed into his eyes, saw his love for her so blatantly expressed there, and almost lost her nerve. She shook her head to clear her clouding thoughts and continued. "Don't start now to tell me how you feel, Dimitri." She wanted to walk away, to put more distance between them. But Dimitri called out to her, his voice desperate.

"Stop Valentina, please! I'm sorry for all the times I teased you, for all the pranks. Maybe I didn't say what I wanted to the right way. I meant that I waited for you to be old enough for a relationship. I just want to be with you. I love you, Valentina." Dimitri's shoulders shook. He could not help but break down now. He felt a sinking feeling in his stomach and a choking sensation burned in his throat. What was happening? They were so happy. What had changed? "We've never conformed to people's ideas of what's proper or acceptable. We've displayed our love for one another and fell in love despite our different backgrounds. You're the one who taught me the value in loving someone for who they are, not what they represent. Whatever it is, whatever's happened, we can get past it. I can't change who

I am. If you run from me, then I have failed in loving you. Please, Valentina, don't leave me for that soldier boy. Please don't break my heart. Please don't leave me," he pleaded, his voice cracking. He tried to swallow past the lump in his throat, but it was impossible.

"How can one forget his heritage or his past?" Valentina argued. Her eyes welled up again as she watched him. Her bottom lip trembled as she fought to compose herself. Did she dare tell him the truth? What would he do with the knowledge that Antonio had raped her? Could she even tell him about their baby? She started to speak, and then paused. It was too late for them. Dimitri's parents, her own family, and the village would never condone their relationship, and she would destroy his life with a child out of wedlock. "Next week I start my journey, and I want you to always remember the words I speak to you today. I already know the result of my decision to end things between us. I have to believe that this expression of pain and sorrow will somehow serve as a curative function later on with the understanding of the detour that our lives are forcing us to take. Wherever we are, we will share in silence our emotions of conflict and misery. I am prevented from loving you because of whispered accusations of who I am, the daughter of a poor housekeeper who has no status in the village. I don't want to hurt you, Dimitri. That's why I have to go. But know that I will always love you, and only you." She turned away from him and started back through the orchard to the hill.

"Valentina, wait." Dimitri ran up to her, the need to touch her again too strong to resist. "I don't know what's going on here. I thought we were happy together, and I know there is more here than you're telling me. I won't pretend that I understand, but at least let me leave you with something to remember me. Even with the passage of years I will never outgrow my love for you.

Part of me is dead, knowing another man will be touching you and holding you every night." The last few words caught in his throat, and Dimitri had to pause before he could finish. "Take this," he offered as he removed a gold chain from around his neck. It was thick and obviously expensive. A small soccer ball charm dangled from it, a gift from Dimitri's father when he had been a boy and just learning how to play. "Wear it and think of me. Maybe one day you can explain all this and we can be happy again. I know I will always remember our time together." He did not hold back his tears, but let them fall down his face as he stared at the only woman he knew he could ever love. She was so beautiful, so perfect in his eyes that Dimitri felt his heart leave him. It would follow Valentina wherever she went. He no longer had any use for it. She was taking all of his love for her with her, and it did not matter.

"Thank you," she whispered as she slipped it over her neck. The chain sparkled in the setting sun, and she tucked it inside her dress. "I do love you," she said as she leaned into him and laid her hands on his chest for support.

Dimitri looked down into her eyes and fought with his feelings. He was furious with her for being so free-spirited. Obviously something had happened to upset her and make her break things off between them. He wondered if perhaps his mother had gotten to her. Why else would she run off and marry some stranger? But another part of him longed to kiss her senseless until she agreed to stay with him forever. He lowered his lips to hers and she raised her head in anticipation of his kiss. He moved his mouth over her soft, warm lips. They created magic with their lips and tongues, a promise of what else could transpire between them if they let their emotions take over.

Valentina abruptly pulled away. If she gave into her passions, she knew she would be lost and unable to carry out her decision.

She took in Dimitri's stunned expression, a sheen of sweat on his handsome face from the heat of their passionate kiss. "I am so sorry," she apologized. Reaching around him, she ran her fingers down the tight curve of his back. Their bodies ached with the need for each other, but she had to leave now, before it would be too late.

Dimitri, unable to find his voice, mouthed the words, "Don't go."

The tears fell like puddles over her upper lip. That last image of Dimitri was the one she would remember forever.

* * *

Dimitri had wanted to make love to her one last time, but he would not have been able to let her go if he had. He wondered at her boldness in touching him, as if she shared his thoughts. But the pain in her eyes left no room for compromise, and so he let her go without that one last chance at pleasure and fulfillment. He watched her pick her way through the orchard, his heart a dead weight in his chest. He would forever mourn Valentina, of that he had no doubt. She had been his light, and that perfection had been forever extinguished. He still did not understand her reasons for saying good-bye, but he would honor her wishes and leave her alone. Dimitri slowly turned away and walked home in the fading sunlight.

* * *

It wasn't until she was well out of Dimitri's sight that Valentina let her guard down and fully accepted the pain she had tried hard to dull while she said good-bye. She cried out, "I am sorry, Dimitri. You are the innocent one in all this. There is so much I could have told you, but this is for the best. I love you." She wanted to know how he felt, wanted to run back to him and take the grief from his eyes. But she had seen the anguish she had placed there. Those blue eyes spoke to her heart every time he looked at her.

It was a while before Valentina realized just how late it had gotten. Her shadow followed as she made her way through an old footpath overgrown with the old woman's blueberries. She quickened her steps as she left the orchard behind. Her mother would be looking for her, and she could not bear to be there any longer, knowing what she had shared with Dimitri under the cover of those fragrant trees. She could never again steal another orange from there. She would leave their special place sacred, and never return.

Chapter 8

There would be serious repercussions with the next decisions she made, Valentina realized as she took off her sister's dress and laid it across her bed. She combed out her hair and sat down, her mind sifting through what she would tell her mother and Ana. There was no other way now. She would have to protect her baby at all costs, and the only way to do that was to give it a father. And that man would have to be Antonio.

The thought made her cringe, but Valentina had no choice. No one else would take her now, especially after they found out she was with child. She would have to sacrifice her dignity and accept Antonio as her husband. She wished with all her heart things could be different, but this was the only way. As she dressed in her regular clothes, Valentina prayed for strength to carry out this new future.

She avoided Ana as long as she could, pretending to be ill whenever she came by. But after a week of refusing to see her friend, Valentina knew she could not put it off any longer. She headed to Ana's house to speak with her, but her mother told her she had gone to the store. Discouraged, Valentina returned home, figuring that Fate decided today was not the day to confront Ana with her news.

In fact, Fate had other plans. As Valentina neared her house, she heard voices coming from the front door. She entered the house, and there sat her mother and Antonio. He stood when she walked in, a twisted smile on his face. "*Bom dia* Valentina," he greeted her. "I have something very important to discuss with you."

She walked into the room slowly, fear gripping her heart. Her mother looked furious, and she noticed her sister sitting behind her, her expression also angry. "Sit down," her mother ordered, and Valentina immediately sat across from her on one of their old benches. "Why did you not tell me that Antonio has been courting you?" she demanded.

"Mama, it's complicated…" Valentina stammered, but her mother cut her off.

"You have been intimate with this man. Do you deny it?" Her voice rose with each word. "Do you?" she shouted when Valentina did not immediately answer.

"No Mama," Valentina whispered. She shot a look to Antonio. He stared back at her with a smug look of triumph. How dare he! Valentina wanted to scream from the unfairness of it all. He had tricked her. His plan all along had been to force Valentina into marrying him. She had been foiled by his deceit, and now there was no other choice. With a weary sigh, she turned to her mother. "We have been intimate Mama." Telling her mother it was rape seemed pointless. Whatever had been said between her and Antonio before Valentina arrived home would outweigh anything she might try to offer in her defense now.

"I see." Valentina's mother stood and paced the length of the tiny room. "And you are also with child?" she asked.

Valentina took a deep breath and again looked at Antonio. He had not told her mother that what happened had only been a week ago. "Yes," she answered.

Antonio's face spoke volumes. The mixture of shock and confusion there slowly transformed into a look of cruel understanding. "You carry *my* child?" he asked. He suddenly questioned his motive for wanting to marry Valentina. Did he really want to bind his life to hers, or did he simply want to break her spirit and force her to choose him? Now it seemed Fate had decided for him.

"I do." Valentina silently begged forgiveness for her lie. But her child needed a father, and there was no way Valentina's mother would allow her to raise the baby alone without a husband at her side.

"Then you will be married as soon as possible." Her mother paused in mid step and turned to Antonio. "When can arrangements be made?"

"Wait! There is no need to rush this!" It was one thing to think of marrying Antonio. It was another to actually go through with it. Valentina shivered as her mother's furious gaze focused on her. "I will not be disgraced by you Valentina. You will marry Antonio and go to his village. There you will raise your child and suffer the shame of breaking God's law by sharing your bed with a man to whom you were not married. I will not support such a disgrace in my house!" She sat abruptly and began to calculate. "We will have the wedding the day after tomorrow. I will speak to the priest myself." She left no room for argument. Valentina felt her world collapse as her mother added, "You will be Mrs. Antonio Fero in two days. Get used to the idea Valentina. You are no longer my daughter, but Antonio's wife."

Valentina couldn't take anymore. She fled the room with her guitar in hand and raced out to the backyard. Her first thought was to hide in the orchard for a while, but she had vowed never to go there again. She knelt on the soft grass and cried, her sobs torn from the depths of her soul. It was all happening too fast. She still needed time to grieve over Dimitri. How could she marry someone else so quickly? She reached for her guitar and started to sing: "Cravo branco, ama ama/no jardim adora adora/eu já tinha outro amor/se tens pena, chora agora."

A noise startled her and she looked up, surprised to find Antonio standing there. He shifted awkwardly from one foot to the other, obviously embarrassed by the state she was in. "I know what I did was wrong," he began.

"You're right, it was." Valentina stood and wiped her eyes. "You are a two-faced, lying bastard. You used me and my closest friend to get what you wanted. Well, now you'll have me, won't you? Me and my child." She fought to keep her anger under control as she faced him down. "In two days I'll be your wife. In the meantime, I want you to leave me alone."

"I'm not stupid Valentina. I know the baby is not mine." He took a step towards her but stopped at her venomous stare. "I will raise it if that's what it takes to have you. I know I have wronged you, but I will be a good husband to you." He sounded so sincere that Valentina wished she could believe him.

"We will see," she replied softly.

* * *

"How could you!" Ana sobbed into her handkerchief, then raised her red-rimmed eyes to the girl she'd once called a friend. "You lied to me! All this time I thought Antonio might come to care for me, but it was all a mean, horrible trick." Her heart was broken. The only true friend she'd ever known had betrayed her. "Why Valentina? You could have had anyone, even Dimitri. Haven't I been a good friend to you?"

Valentina dried her own eyes before answering. "You've always been good to me Ana. But I finally saw Antonio for who he really was, and we fell in love." She almost choked on the last part, but these days lying came so easily to her that Valentina continued, "You'll find someone better, believe me." *Yes you will,* she added silently, *far better than that scoundrel.*

Valentina turned away from Ana, suddenly unable to face her. For years they'd been as sisters, sharing in each other's joys and sorrows. Ana had always been able to turn to her when the women in the village were especially cruel, or when Ana wasn't getting along with her mother. And Valentina had always known she could do the same. Two friends could not have been closer, but now Valentina had committed the worst possible betrayal. She knew in the long run she would be doing Ana a great favor, but her friend would never know that.

"Valentina." She turned to find Ana's cold, lifeless eyes trained on her.

"I hate you!" Ana nearly screamed as she stood and headed for the door. She yanked it open and cried out, "Get out of my house! I never want to see you again!"

"Ana, please…" Valentina begged, but Ana stood firm, one hand on the door and another over her heart. "You have hurt me beyond measure, Valentina Marques. Good-bye."

Valentina rose from her chair and left. She did not spare Ana one last glance. *So be it*, she decided. Ana did not know that she had just been spared from a loveless life with Antonio. She shook her head as she mourned her lost friendship. In only a week, she'd lost the man she loved and her only true friend. Valentina let her tears fall as she walked home. These days all she could do was cry. Tomorrow was her wedding day. It promised to be the worst day of her life.

* * *

Ana sat quietly, her heart torn into a million pieces. Valentina had done the one thing she had always feared. She had stolen the man Ana loved.

Part of her understood that she was no match for Valentina's looks and charms, but she did feel guilty for the hidden resentment she felt towards Valentina. Now she questioned whether she was being punished for this. Sometimes she wished Valentina had scars on her face or that her smile would reveal crooked teeth, or even that her clothes weren't so bright and colorful. Thinking of Valentina's liveliness brought pain into the pit of her stomach every time, much like the pain she felt when she looked at her own mother's life.

She'd lived in deceit and denial all her life, trying to convince herself that she could be as outgoing as her friend or beautiful like her mother. Ana knew her mother wanted to marry her off and be rid of the last reminder of her old life. But there were only a few men left in the village who weren't spoken for, and Ana knew that if she was not engaged by the end of the year, her mother would most likely bribe one of them to marry her and take her away. She'd even made sure Ana's hand in marriage came with a very generous dowry.

Ana's otherwise boring life would shine in Valentina's company. Her plain face would glow with excitement no matter where they went. Just the sight of Valentina with her guitar slung over her shoulder would draw people to ask her to stop and sing a song. Most of the time Valentina would seek out the company of the old man who used to sit with his back against the tavern wall, a stick between his legs that he was carving into a cane with his pocketknife. Valentina would sit next to him while he chiseled away at his project and fine tune her guitar. He would always ask her to sing the same song before she left, *My Mother's Shawl.*

Ana would sit and listen like the other villagers, marveling at how one person could have such command over so many. But that was Valentina, she conceded as tears threatened to fall.

Valentina could have anything and anyone she wanted. Ana could have what she discarded, and that was supposed to be enough.

"I will never forgive you," Ana spat out as she watched Valentina walk home. This time Valentina would not have what she wanted.

Chapter 9

She waited by the front door for Antonio. Valentina looked down at her dress, borrowed for the wedding because there had been no time to make one. She held a bouquet of pale blue hydrangeas, not at all the white roses she'd hoped for. Everything about this wedding went against her wishes, from the food to the location. She did not want to marry in her village. She couldn't face committing to one man while the one she truly loved was only a few streets away. But Antonio had insisted. "We will marry here before we leave for my village," he'd told Valentina and her mother. "We will have a small celebration here, then a grand one in my village where you will meet all of my family and friends."

Valentina closed her eyes as the sting of tears threatened once again. Her life was spinning out of control. She was about to enter into holy matrimony with a man she did not love. Even the wedding wasn't going to be at all like the one she'd planned when daydreaming about Dimitri. She wasn't even allowed to wear her hair down. Valentina's mother had braided her hair and coiled it on her head. It was confining and uncomfortable, much like the day would be. She wiped away a stray tear. Her old life had ended, and this new one already seemed destined to extinguish her spirit.

A knock at the door scattered her thoughts, and she opened it to find Antonio, in full uniform, ready to take her to the church. He looked her over appreciatively. "You look breathtaking," he smiled.

"Thank you." She swept past him to the waiting open cart. He followed behind her and aided her as Valentina climbed up into the seat. Antonio climbed up and settled next to her, then sent the horse into a trot as they slowly rode through the village.

Well-wishers lined the main road that led to the church. The ceremony itself was short and unremarkable. Valentina could not even remember what the priest had said. The only sign she had of actually being married was the thin gold band now adorning the ring finger of her left hand. Even the ring had been borrowed. She'd spoken her vows and kissed her new husband as though it were all happening to someone else. The only thing that got her through the entire ordeal were thoughts of her baby, of Dimitri's baby. She was not yet showing, one of the reasons the wedding was so sudden. But throughout the day, Valentina would place a hand over her belly and remind herself why she had gone through with this. "For you, my sweet baby," she whispered.

Antonio was every inch the besotted groom. He paid careful attention to her the entire day. She had never had to ask for a drink or something to eat. He automatically brought it before she could voice the thought. He'd planned a small celebration at her house for her family and friends, a smaller group now that Ana and her mother were not coming. Valentina smiled and tried her best to be cheerful. She studied her new husband, his eyes as dark as midnight when he would look at her. The firm set of his jaw and straight, full lips sharpened his features, and she admitted he was rather attractive. *I will learn to love him,* she hoped. It was all she could do.

* * *

It was as Valentina made another sweep of the backyard to greet their guests that she saw him. Her heart flip-flopped in her chest as she saw Dimitri enter the gate. He looked dashing in a dark suit and crisp white shirt. His blue eyes raked over her, his gaze fierce and possessive. Valentina wanted nothing more than to run straight into his arms, but she held her emotions in check. She was Mrs. Antonio Fero now, whether she liked it or not.

"*Bom dia* Valentina," Dimitri said as he came up to her. "I just wanted to congratulate you on your happy day." She noted that he looked tired and worn down. Dark circles smudged his eyes, but he was still the most handsome man she had ever laid eyes on. "So I lost out to the soldier boy?" he teased.

Valentina smiled half-heartedly and replied, "I may have married Antonio, but I gave myself to you. Never forget that."

"I know." His hands shook as he took her by the arms. He kissed her lightly on the cheek and said his good-byes. "Be well Valentina. I hope this is everything you wanted."

Valentina took each of his hands and kissed each one, smudging them with tears. Dimitri gently wiped the streaming tears from her cheeks. He drew away from her and extended his hand to shake Antonio's, who had come to stand protectively by his wife when he spotted Dimitri talking to her. "Congratulations. I hope you're both very happy together."

"We will be. Of that I have no doubt." Antonio smiled coldly at his rival and wrapped an arm around Valentina's waist. Dimitri did not miss the involuntary jerk as Valentina reacted to her husband's touch, but he said nothing. It was too late anyhow. She was a married woman now, and his heart would always be lost to her.

"Farewell Valentina," he said. Through puffed and damp eyes that hadn't slept in days, he watched the woman that he knew he would spend the rest of his life trying to forget pull away from him, her heart given to another. With a last, sad smile, Dimitri walked out of the gate and disappeared from view.

"Farewell." Valentina looked at Antonio and said, "We need to see to the other guests." She would not let him see her pain.

But Antonio did not let her go immediately. He leaned over and kissed her. "You have nothing to fear from me," he reassured her. "I will take care of you."

"I know you will," she replied. He looked so sincere that she felt guilty not believing in him. "I will be a good wife to you." She would put her destiny in God's hands now.

He smiled and led her over to the food table, his mind on only one thought: *I will put the fear of God into her now.*

* * *

Valentina lay in bed, ashamed and disgusted with herself. She had willingly given herself to Antonio this time. He was her husband now, and had demanded his husbandly rights. She'd shut her eyes as he'd touched her, unable to look at his face and know that it wasn't Dimitri making love to her. It sickened her to know she had betrayed him in this way, but there was no other choice. What could she do now? She had decided that Dimitri couldn't possibly want her after what had happened, and she had decided that Antonio would have to become her husband. Her baby needed a father, and while she knew Dimitri would have gladly wed her and raised their son, he would have been shunned by his family and the village. His medical career would have suffered, and it would all be her fault. "I'm so sorry," she whispered as she closed her hand around the pendant at her neck. She cried herself to sleep, her thoughts on Dimitri.

* * *

Dimitri sat in the orchard, staring up at the stars. He'd given his heart to Valentina here, promised to love her forever. What had changed? Why had she married Antonio Fero? He shook his head, unable to fathom what her reason could have been. He thought of how she'd looked at her wedding, a vision that took his breath away, and it made him want to break Fero's neck for stealing her away from him. He also thought of her in that bastard's bed, and his hands on Dimitri's woman. "No!" It was an anguished cry, torn from the deepest part of his soul. He had thought their happiness was guaranteed, as permanent as the stars that blurred before his eyes. He would have done anything for her, even if it meant going against his family so they could be together. But something had made Valentina rethink their relationship. Didn't she trust in his love for her? What more could he have done?

Dimitri sighed as he uncorked the wine bottle lying next to him. There was only one way to pass this night, he decided as he took a large swallow from the bottle.

Chapter 10

Valentina packed her satchel with the few articles of clothing she had. She had returned to her mother's house to gather her things and say good-bye. It seemed that all she did lately was bid farewell to the ones she loved. As time neared, she tried to force an optimistic attitude. Voicing her thoughts, she said, "I always wanted to travel to other villages and meet new people. The difficult part will not be the journey itself, but making the journey with the man who had betrayed me and taken advantage of me."

Her mother walked into the room just as Valentina snapped her bag closed. "Are you ready?" she asked. "Antonio is waiting outside."

"I'm coming," she replied, too preoccupied to notice that her mother remained in the doorway.

"I have something for you," her mother said.

Valentina turned and saw that her mother carried a shawl in one hand. It was dark and heavy, inappropriate for the time of year. "Thank you Mama," she said, a bit confused over the gift.

"Wear this on your journey Valentina. You are a married woman now, and you must act like one." She indicated the braids pinned to her daughter's head and added, "That is part of your identity now. You are no longer the free-spirited girl that ran loose in the village. Perhaps I should have taken a firmer hand with you. But that does not matter now. You must never dishonor your husband. Always listen to him and obey what he says. He requested I give you this shawl so that you may cover yourself on the journey to your new home. Do not disappoint me Valentina."

"I won't Mama." Inside Valentina was screaming. First her hair, and now this? Was her married life to begin with such confinement? "But I don't see why…" she tried, but her mother held up a hand and cut her off.

"Do not disappoint me," she repeated. She spread the shawl out on the bed and left the room. Valentina stared at it, her mind rebelling at this invasion of her freedom. She draped the shawl around her shoulders and took a last look in the mirror. She looked like every other married woman in the village now. The thought made her want to cry out in frustration at such unfairness, but she stopped herself. She would not cry this day. Whatever she had to do as she began her new life, she would do it. This was no longer simply about her, but her baby as well.

Antonio waited for her in the open cart, but she noted that this time he did not make a move to help her up. She climbed up into the seat and adjusted her shawl when she saw his disapproving gaze. *And so it begins,* she sighed as they rolled away from her home. She looked back and saw her sister watching from the front window. She gave a slight wave, and Valentina waved back, her heart aching for the life she was leaving behind. Antonio said casually, "You don't need to worry about them anymore. Your life is with me now."

Valentina frowned at him. "My mother did not even say good-bye." She searched the house for signs of her, but she was nowhere in sight. Valentina gave up and turned around in her seat. Her old life was behind her now. She glanced at Antonio's sharp profile, and felt her heart break a little more. Her life was with him now, and this was the path she had to follow.

"Pull your shawl up over your hair," he suggested, but Valentina heard the hint of command in his voice. "Married women should not show themselves to any passing stranger."

A retort waited on the tip of her tongue, but Valentina chose to keep silent. Why anger him? They were only one day into their marriage, and his village was still a good distance away. The trip would be unpleasant enough without the added discomfort of an argument between them. She pulled the shawl over her hair and crossed in it front of her as she had seen the older women in the village do. The sun beat down on her head, but it would be better to suffer the heat's wrath than Antonio's. She sensed that he would be a force to be reckoned with if he got angry.

They rode in silence for hours, the countryside a blur as Valentina's thoughts were always on Dimitri. What was he doing? Did he miss her? Would he grieve for her as she did for him? Part of her wanted him to forget about what they'd shared. The pain would lessen over time and he would find someone else to love. But another part of her could not consider that he might find love again one day. What would she do if she learned he had married someone else?

Antonio had been speaking to her, but she had to ask him to repeat what he'd said. "What are you thinking about?"

"Nothing really, just our new life and our new home," Valentina lied.

"Really? It seemed to me that you might be thinking of your precious Dimitri." Antonio slowed the cart and looked at her, his eyes dangerous in the light of the setting sun. "Understand this, Valentina. You made your choice. You could have had Dimitri Maciel, but you picked me. And I will not let you go." As if to prove his claim on her, he pulled her against him and kissed her roughly. She fought to pull away, but his grip was too strong. He plundered her mouth with his tongue, and Valentina again felt fearful that she should not anger him. She kissed him back, furious with herself for being such a weakling. She could not stand up to him. Her baby's life was too important to her.

Antonio pulled away, a satisfied smile spreading across his face. "That's the kind of response I'll expect the next time I kiss you. Be the wife you should be." He flicked the reins and they began to move again. He did not say another word to her until they reached an inn. He slowed the cart and leaped down to tie the donkey to a nearby tree. Valentina moved to climb down but he stopped her. "You stay here. I'll get food for us."

Valentina watched as he disappeared into the inn. She felt hurt and angry, and there was nothing she could do. He did not allow her off the cart until he had found a secluded spot underneath some trees where they could eat. "Why can't we eat inside?" she asked as she tried to make herself comfortable on the rocky ground.

Antonio looked up from the sandwiches he had bought and froze her with his stare. "Because I said so," he replied.

They passed the night at another inn several miles away, just as midnight approached. Valentina tossed and turned on the narrow bed, unable to sleep. The only affection Antonio had shown her today was a demand that she be intimate with him before he fell asleep. Except that the act was only to please him and not her as well. Valentina tried to wipe away the memory of his body over hers, his hands rough and unsteady because of the wine he'd had with their supper. She wanted to cry, since it was all she seemed to do anymore. But the tears would not come. She had shed all she could when she said good-bye to her life, and now the tears that would come next would be saved for her new home. She suspected there would be a great need for them there.

They started early the next morning, well before the other travelers were up for the day. Antonio had bought cheese and bread for their trip, not wanting to stop again until they were near his village. The journey was quiet and uneventful. They stopped only to attend to their personal needs. Valentina had to keep her head covered at all times, and again they ate under the protection of the trees when mealtimes came. She felt isolated and rejected. She was good enough for Antonio to mount each night like a dog in heat, but she could not be seen with her own husband in public. She lightly touched the braids pinned to her head. She had let them down the night before, only to hear Antonio retort, "I never want to see your hair down again Valentina. You are not the loose girl you once were. You're my wife now, and I will say how you'll wear your hair."

Anything she did to displease him brought an angry comment from Antonio. As they finally neared his village some hours later, he pulled her close and muttered, "Do as I say and this will all go easy for you. Do not disappoint me Valentina," he warned, an echo of her mother's last words to her.

Valentina observed the workers in the fields, some gathering the corn and wheat crops, others piling the harvest into baskets and wagons. She admired the fertile landscape, and wondered if she might be happy here one day. "All of these people work for you?" she asked Antonio.

He looked at her a moment, then slowly replied, "Yes, they all work for me."

His statement left her somewhat unsettled, but she said nothing. They were coming upon a modest stone house that resembled many of the scattered homes they'd passed on their journey. As they slowed to a stop in the small front yard, several women ran outside to greet them. Antonio helped her down from the cart, once again the model husband. "Mother, meet my wife, Valentina," he said.

The stocky woman before her sized Valentina up and

wrinkled her nose. "Welcome to our family," she declared, but Valentina realized the smile on the older woman's face was not genuine. "These are Antonio's sisters and sisters-in-law." She quickly introduced the other women to her, and they all gave her cold, detached smiles. Valentina felt like a mouse caught between a wall and several hungry cats. They took their time studying her. Valentina suddenly felt the need to say something, anything to cut the tension that was quickly building in the small yard.

"I was surprised to see so many of Antonio's employees out in the fields today. It must be very warm out there." She tried to smile politely at Mrs. Fero, but the older woman frowned at her.

"Antonio's employees? Oh, you mean my husband. Yes, it is warm today, but the boys will be fine." She glanced at her son, who had paled visibly at Valentina's question. "All of Antonio's family work for my husband, including Antonio when he is not in service. My son is very amusing. He told you he owned the fields. Even we don't own the fields. We simply rent them." The other women laughed, but Valentina felt sick to her stomach. He'd lied to her again, and there was no way out for her now. Reluctantly she let Antonio take her hand and together they walked into the house, not his but his parents'. It seemed nothing about Antonio Fero had been true after all, and the poverty she had left behind had followed her to this new home.

In fact, this new home was just like the one she had left behind. Valentina felt the blood rush to her face. Her chest felt as tight as an encased sausage. She silently asked for super human strength to hold her tongue. She wrapped her arms protectively around her waist and frowned as she glanced from side to side, disappointment etched on her face. "So this is my punishment," she whispered.

Chapter 11

Bread making was definitely the worst of the many new tasks she had to learn, Valentina thought bitterly as she rubbed the small of her back. It was tedious and dull, especially for someone who was four months pregnant and on her feet all day. After she'd knead the dough, she had to cover the bowl with a cloth, then a wooden cover. It was placed in the stone oven to stay warm and rise. This process was repeated until there were enough loaves to last a week. She looked around at the flour-dusted bowls and pans. She still had a long way to go.

Antonio's mother, although rather suspicious and distrustful of her since she arrived, had taken on the role of teacher. Valentina was the only one of the Fero women not allowed out in the fields to work, and so the older woman had begun showing her the household chores, one by one. At first Valentina had protested. She wanted to be outside with the others, enjoying the fresh air and the sense of being useful. But Antonio had been firm. "I will not only tame you," he'd said the first night they'd spent in his home, "but you will learn to be the best wife in this village. Singing is a thing of your youth. Your guitar will be put away and you will only play it on Sundays after mass." Singing and laughter had been a vital part of Valentina's life, but she did neither now. And when Antonio did not verbally torment her with his threats and dire promises, he would use his hands.

This was how her married life had begun. She thought that by now she might feel some affection towards her new husband, but the only emotion Valentina had in abundance was fear. That and an increasing dislike for his demanding and nosy family who always seemed to know what she was doing and constantly meddled in her business.

Valentina sighed as she pulled her shawl over her head. The rest of the bread would have to wait until tomorrow. Antonio had told her that morning that they were going on an outing, the first since they'd been married. She watched him roll into the yard, perched on the seat of the open donkey-drawn cart. Valentina's hopes of him reaching a hand down to help her up were diminished as he instead fussed with the wooden pails he'd brought along. She thought that odd, but said nothing as they rode away.

The trip was silent, much like the way they'd been living lately. When Antonio did bother to speak with her, she usually wished he wouldn't. Valentina had become accustomed to the routine. They ate breakfast under a shady tree some ways down the road. She had been allowed to remove her shawl, a blessing since her head felt as if it were on fire. She idly wondered what sort of adventure Antonio had planned. The road they had been traveling was quite long and they had been driving for quite a while. It felt like hours had passed when he finally turned the cart onto a small dirt path. There were no houses, only plants and trees of all shapes and sizes. They passed near a cornfield as they continued further. It was the best part of the day so far, Valentina decided as she heard the corn click and whisper beautiful sounds in the wind. She loved to listen to nature's language.

Antonio finally stopped the cart and said, "Get out. It's time to work." He pointed to a corner of the cart and ordered, "Take that sackcloth and spread it on the cart bed. We're going to dig up *inhamos*. First we'll fill the pails. Those are for my mother." He handed her a pail, kept one for him, and led the way through the thick trees.

Valentina was speechless. This was their outing? She hated digging up those bland root vegetables, but it was Antonio's favorite food. Her brain screamed in protest. She had been tricked again by her deceiving husband. Hot fluid gathered in the back of her throat, and she had to struggle to swallow. But something deep within her had long since resigned itself to the life she now led. As if to remind her of why her choice had been this one, the baby fluttered in her belly.

She thought Antonio would at least have the courtesy to hold the tree branches while she trudged her way through the overgrown greens that covered the narrow footpath. But it was all a sick game to him. Antonio would hold a branch, steal a look back at her, and then release it as she struggled to hold on to it to avoid being struck. *Dimitri would never have done this to me*, she thought bitterly as one particularly heavy branch caught her in the forehead and left a scratch.

Her eyes welled up with tears as she remembered other walks through the woods as a child. Dimitri would always lead the way to pick wild berries. He would take her arm in his and he always held the branches. He also waited for her, unlike Antonio who marched ahead without a second look at her, unless he was playing one of his mean tricks. She would look up into Dimitri's sparkling blues eyes. "Watch your head," he would often remind her so she would not be hurt by the low hanging branches. Her heart ached with longing for him and for those simpler days. Valentina knew it wasn't right to compare them to each other, but she couldn't help it. It had been a very long time since anyone had spoken a simple, kind word to her. She was an outsider here, and everyone made sure to remind her every chance they got.

At last they reached the large patch of *inhamos*. Valentina surveyed the ground before her and made up her mind. She was going to survive in this unwelcoming village and in her unhappy marriage. And the only place to start was with Antonio. She attempted to say something to please him, even though the words weren't quite from her heart. "I know I have a lot to learn. I promise I'll work very hard and I'll be a good wife to you."

Antonio studied her, his eyes lingering a little longer than they usually did these days. "Yes, you will work hard," he finally replied, "since you didn't have any trouble chasing your pig Jorge into the woods, where you'd meet Dimitri."

She felt as though he had struck her. How did he know about her childhood games with Dimitri? Defensively she replied, "That is not true. Jorge would wander off into the woods and get lost. Dimitri would help me find him." She looked away from him and nervously smoothed out the wrinkles in her skirt. Antonio looked ready to kill her.

His chest tightened with the need to strike out at her. "No one thought you'd give me a second look," he spat out. "You thought you were so high and mighty with your singing voice and guitar playing. I don't know why I ever married you. I wonder why I went through with such a foolish idea. I'm really sorry I did. I resent the fact that you thought you were too good for me." He took a deep breath and readied for another attack, but she cut him off.

"I'm subjected to the physical obligations that accompany the marriage vows, but I endure it all in silence," she said to him. "I know you don't love me, Antonio. You use me to satisfy yourself because it's convenient and simple that way. But today I have found my voice and I'm speaking from the depths of my soul. We are similar in our weaknesses: you for my affection and me for the love of another. You beat me and control me, but it's only your weakness that comes through. But it doesn't matter what you do. It only strengthens me to continue to be unique and true to who I really am." Valentina took an involuntary step back. She knew she walked a very dangerous line in being so forward with Antonio, but part of her no longer cared. It was about time she told him how she really felt.

"You bring on your own misery and grief," she continued, her confidence growing as she noticed him lower his eyes to the ground, his expression unreadable. "When we got married, the symbolism of the ceremony was the joining of our souls. But the cruelest thing that could have happened actually came to pass. We've become split souls. I thought we could make a life together. You proclaimed to love me, but that was really your hate and jealousy that masqueraded as your love for me." Valentina dropped her pail on the ground and wrapped her arms around her waist. Antonio did not miss the gesture and took a step towards her.

"Always protecting that bastard baby, aren't you? We have work to do, so I think your little tirade is over." He stooped and began to work at the ground with his hands, pulling up the small root vegetables and dropping them into the pail.

Valentina knelt down and caught his gaze. "I'm not finished," she said.

"Yes you are Valentina. Don't make me angry," he warned, his eyes cold as they bore into hers. "Now get to work."

"You were jealous Antonio," she said by way of reply. When he didn't speak, she went on. "You were jealous of my love for Dimitri, and that's why you raped me." She noted that he cringed at her mention of the rape, and it spurred her on. "It was your way of taking away my pride. You forced me to surrender my individuality, and to surrender to your desire. It was an act of aggression," she accused. "You took by force what was given freely to another. That's how you punished me for loving Dimitri. How can you love and hate me at the same time? Instead of coming to you freely, out of love, you force me into a submissive role." She took in his expression and sighed. "You look frustrated with me Antonio. Your struggle between love and hate and it will be the death of you."

Antonio rose up to his full height and angrily wiped his hands on his thighs. He pinned her with his stare and shouted, "Why do you insist on provoking me? I said I'd put the fear of God into you, but still you push me!" He grabbed her by the arm and forced her to stand, smiling in satisfaction as he saw her lip tremble with fear. She couldn't help but look into his dark, haunted eyes, and found her courage there.

She jerked her arm free, her own eyes now flat and devoid of warmth as cold steel. "By doing what you did you condemned me to hell!" she cried out. "But the pride I cling to is that I carry Dimitri's baby."

"You're a fool if you think Dimitri loved you," Antonio spat at her. "He was there to amuse himself, not to court you. Rich men don't court housekeepers' daughters."

"You'll never understand the love we shared," she answered cryptically.

Antonio fell silent, his expression filled with disgust. He would not lower himself to reason with her, or show that he cared what she thought of him. Valentina was his wife, not Dimitri's, and she would come around to his way of thinking, whether she wanted to or not.

Valentina made it through the rest of the day in a blur of emotions, from terror at what Antonio might do to her, to pride for speaking up at last. In the days and nights that followed, she would lie on her uncomfortable cornhusk mattress and think of all that she'd lost. She'd pretend to be asleep as she thought of

Dimitri. "What have I done, Dimitri?" she wondered miserably. "I want to feel your strong arms around me. I betrayed you by not telling you that you were going to be a father." Tears would begin to fall as she thought of their brief but magical time together. "I'll always remember the passion we shared, and my heart belongs to you. I may share a house with Antonio, but not my heart. I suffer my misery in silence."

Chapter 12

Valentina was determined to make Antonio's home her home, and she would pretend he actually cared about her. She started with dressing to please him. She put on a dress her mother-in-law had given her, and with great pride she'd tell him that she had made it. It fell loosely on her body, hiding her curves. She accented her dutiful wife look with her hair. The two long braids came away from the center part, crisscrossed in back of her head and met again on the top center like a wreath, then looped down again. She kept herself busy cleaning their little rented house and cooking supper as she waited for her husband. Antonio's mother checked up on her and said, "That's the way I like seeing you Valentina. My son works very hard to put food on the table." She inspected the tidy surroundings and sniffed at the delicious aroma coming from the hearth. "It looks like you don't need me around to help you." Thankfully, she went off for a nap and left Valentina in peace for the rest of the day. Valentina could now go outside for an hour and mingle with the other women and get to know them. As evening approached, she practiced a new song that she would sing for Antonio. Maybe if she pretended to love him, they could live in peace: "Ai vem o meu amor/ele ai vem chegando/as botas lhe vem renjindo/mas que graça lhe vem dando." She smiled at herself and said, "Not bad." She was getting good at pretending. "Let me put another one together," she thought. "Cara linda, cara linda/cara linda, bem te vejo/quem me dera cara linda/no teu rosta dar um bejo."

But it seemed like her best efforts were in vain. The front door flew open and she jumped out of her seat. She gripped her hands together to keep calm, but she was terrified. Antonio staggered into the house. God help her, she had never seen him this drunk. He dragged himself towards her and with one arm swung it across the table, sending her carefully prepared supper crashing to the floor. She tried to back away from him, but he yanked her against him and ground out, "Just who are you trying to impress?" He sounded as mean as he looked when he slurred, "I swear to God I'm going to kill you." He shoved her against the wall and slapped her hard across the face. She could feel the blood trickling from her nose and lip. She knew she had to stop this now or he really would kill her and the baby.

Thinking of the tiny life inside of her flooded Valentina with courage, and she cried out, "You will not kill me!" The force of her voice stunned them both. "I swear to you that if you continue to shove and beat me, I'll leave! I rather suffer the shame and go back to my mother. You're a pitiful fool if you think you can wash your insecurities away with alcohol!" She moved a safe distance away from him, edging her way to the door, just in case. "You can't force me to love you! You think that by hitting me you're punishing me. You just want revenge on me because I've stained our marriage with my baby, but you cheat me out of the fullness of married life too! You want me to fear you, but in spite of your abuse, I endure." She took a calming breath and said what she'd wanted to tell him from the first moment of their marriage. "You have to respect my independence and separate existence from you. Don't be concerned with your love for me. Worry about loving yourself first."

Antonio stared at her, confused. "People adored your singing, and that was your purpose." He stumbled over his words. "You had many suitors come calling, and that's how you entertained yourself. You made fools out of all of us."

Valentina studied him a moment, this drunk, hostile man she had the misfortune to call her husband. She found her voice and replied, "Your anxieties destroy any chance that I could love you. You treat me like a leper, keeping me locked up with your mother watching everything I do. You've allowed everyone to think I can't be trusted. Your neighbors measure me by a yardstick, like hanging judges condemning the damned. But you're afraid to admit any shame or guilt for what you did to me." Her voice rose with each accusation. "You won't dominate me or make me suffer anymore!" Valentina was shouting now, her strength restored. Antonio would not make a fool of her again.

But her husband sneered at her and casually remarked, "There is meaning to the marriage vows, Valentina. A bride should be a virgin."

Hurt and shamed by that one statement, Valentina turned and climbed up to the loft to go to sleep. Supper was a ruined mess on the floor, and she found she no longer had any appetite. As she reached the top of the stairs, she looked back at Antonio and replied evenly, "But you married me anyway, didn't you?"

Her words had the desired effect. She would not be ashamed of her baby when he knew very well she was pregnant before he decided to marry her. Antonio's expression was furious, but he kept silent. She went to bed and a while later he joined her, too drunk and tired to demand his husbandly rights tonight. The only noise in the small house was the crunching of the cornhusks beneath them. Only when Valentina was certain that Antonio had turned his back on her and that his breathing was deep and even did she allow her tears to flow freely. It wasn't fair that she should live like this, she thought miserably. She'd hoped for a decent life for herself and the baby, but the reality of her existence only made her cry harder. Her tears puddled on her pillowcase as she fell into a troubled and restless sleep.

* * *

Valentina awoke the next morning, exhausted. She noticed purple smudges under her eyes as she passed Antonio's shaving mirror. They made her look very old and worn down. She went downstairs, surprised to find the supper mess cleaned up and disposed of. Antonio must have done it before he left, she realized. She didn't know whether to be grateful or afraid of the gesture. Valentina walked the length of the house and took in her meager surroundings. She desperately tried to think of one good reason why she should confine herself to the house all day, but couldn't think of one. She had to get out into the fresh air before the walls closed in on her. Antonio's constant demands on her had made Valentina forget her true self. She needed to run free and escape the confinement her marriage had become, if only for one day. Valentina hurried out the door before Antonio's mother could come by and watch her the whole day, and before she lost her nerve.

Antonio left at the crack of dawn each day, and she did not expect him back until after sundown. If she waited around any longer, Antonio's mother would soon be there. She was a prisoner in her own home. Soon she would hear the voices of the hawkers selling their wares, and the fisherman selling the early morning catch, *cavala, sharros,* and *sardinhas.*

Valentina planned out her day. She would first visit the village seamstress and offer to work for free so she could better learn the trade. Her plan was to keep busy in the morning so she could make a good impression on her mother-in-law. The old woman napped in the afternoon, and if she thought Valentina was well occupied with her household chores, then she would be able to get away. They guarded her like a princess, even though she was no one special.

Valentina let her thoughts wander, her mind a jumble of ideas and thoughts. She wanted so much to follow a routine like the rest of the villagers, but she also wanted her freedom. She would keep up her morning routine, the pretense designed to fool her mother-in-law into thinking Valentina would be too tired by the afternoon to possibly get into any mischief or leave the house.

She draped the shawl over her head and around her shoulders, looking very much like the other women of the village. Behind the cover of the shawl she smiled because no one recognized her. Today was her day, and no one would ruin it for her. Running up the small slope behind the house, and eager to make it over the top without being noticed, she kicked off her shoes. Next came the shawl, casually tossed aside in the grass. She took in the beauty of the land, land she had not been allowed to see until now. It was plentiful with blueberries, grapes, and so many different kinds of trees. She decided to follow the path and she'd watch the sun so she would know when to start back home. She discovered another path off the one she traveled and followed it. The landscape before her immediately froze her with its splendor. She enjoyed the deep color of the forest, the rich greens, yellows and reds. Her senses came alive with the different shades that glowed in the sun. Even the simple sounds of nature lured her with their sweet music, the rustling leaves and chirping birds a gentle lullaby to her anxious mind. The colorful hydrangeas and the delicate scent of the wildflowers around her reminded Valentina that she needed to let go of her anxieties and muscle tension. There was no one else here except her, no one to interrupt the tranquility of the day or ruin her brief grasp at freedom. The perfect morning soothed her soul. She realized it took strength to hold on to and go after dreams. Lives have been destroyed by other people's pursuits of money and climbing the social ladder. It was a situation she was all too familiar with, and Valentina smiled at her courage. The risk was great that Antonio's mother could wake up early or someone could come looking for her, but Valentina didn't care. She was too happy in this peaceful place to let the outside world interfere.

She wanted to stay in the forest forever, but she knew she would have to leave before nightfall, and regress to her life outside of this sacred retreat. Valentina squatted down and rested her back against the trunk of a birch tree. She closed her eyes and listened to the snapping twigs with a smile, tilting her head to one side and remembering all the days she spent with Dimitri in the woods, especially the night she gave herself to him in the orchard. The memories brought back all the feelings she felt for him. She remembered not being afraid of what they were about to do. She'd trembled at his touch, and his hands left a tingling warmth lingering on her body. That night she'd known they would always be connected.

With a sigh she stood and brushed at her skirt. It didn't do any good to spend too much time wondering about her lost love. Valentina continued with her exploration of the forest, and soon came to the edge of a plateau beyond some trees that seemed out of place in the dense greenery. Stone steps led down into a grassy clearing. In front of her a natural faucet of water sprung out of a stone wall. Strangest of all was the figure crouched before it, cupping her hands and taking a drink. *She looks so much like me,* Valentina thought as she took in the scene before her. She rubbed her eyes to make sure the woman didn't disappear. Her long, straight brown hair flowed loosely, just like hers once did.

Valentina decided to approach the woman, who jumped

when she heard a noise behind her. "Who are you?" the woman asked, wary. "How did you know of this place?" Recognition suddenly dawned on her and she amended, "Oh, I know who you are! You're the new girl in *Furnas*, Antonio Fero's wife. I've heard all about you. My name is Gabriela." She seemed so kind and genuinely friendly that Valentina had to smile. "I'm Valentina," she replied.

They quickly discovered they had much in common. "My husband Ernesto treats me as badly as yours does," Gabriela confided. At Valentina's embarrassed look, she quickly added, "Don't be embarrassed! It's not your fault. We're the talk of the village, you know. I'm an outsider too," she said conspiratorially. "I came here from *Povoação*, convinced I was in love and desperate to leave home." She suddenly giggled. "The village women think we're going to set a bad example with our loose ways and corrupt everybody."

Valentina laughed until her belly ached. "I didn't know that!" she managed to say. It felt wonderful to be able to talk to someone whose last name wasn't Fero. She felt a kinship with this woman, a fellow alien in a life she had not counted on. She shared her feelings and emotions with her friend. "My husband can't accept me. My moods, impulses, and personal traits mean nothing to him. I'm enslaved by his attitude. I want to live with him in love, a relatedness love that we as human beings have towards one another." She looked doubtful but smiled in spite of it. "But I still hold on to the hope that one day my struggle will end and he will love me for me."

Gabriela nodded her head in understanding. "I know exactly how you feel. Here we have freedom from our misery. This place is where I escape to when life becomes too overwhelming. We can share in it together, Valentina. We don't have to feel like outsiders here. There's no need to pretend with each other. To the villagers, everything we do is tinged with imperfections. To us, we wouldn't have it any other way," she grinned.

* * *

The sun was low in the sky when Valentina realized she had to leave. She said good-bye to her new friend. The hug they shared was filled with the promise to return. Gabriela's rich brown eyes filled with tears as she said, "I've found my twin. You're a reflection of me, and I'm so glad to have met you today." She warned Valentina to keep to the path so she wouldn't lose her way home. "Good-bye Valentina," she called out as she headed the opposite way to her side of the village. Valentina waved her own good-bye, marveling at her good fortune. She started back towards home, her heart light and carefree. Gabriela was so much like her. It was wonderful to know she wasn't alone anymore.

Valentina tried her best to follow the trail, but she knew she was lost. She desperately walked in and out of a trail that was twisted and tangled with trees. She lifted her dress to walk through the thick, overgrown grass, and with every step she took she felt her heart pound in fear. She came to a fork in the path, but she didn't remember seeing it before. She thought to retrace her steps, but found she had gone around in a circle. The sun had set, casting dark, threatening shadows from the trees. She looked up into them, their long, spidery branches waving high into the sky, and the forest appeared even darker under the heavy canopy of leaves. She froze as she faced the presence of real danger. Lost in the menacing woods, she felt like a hunted doe, and her nagging conscience made her ashamed of her impulsive behavior. Valentina thought she would die of fright if she did not find her way out of the forest. The thought of spending the night there made her panic, and she tried to take a deep breath to calm herself.

She faced a great, sheltering oak. Instinctively she craved survival, and after a moment's debate began to climb. At least within the safety of the tree Valentina could escape from the threat of the forest. She missed her foothold and lost her grip. She struggled to grab hold but instead she hit the bumpy ground with a thud. Stunned, she checked herself for injuries. She thought briefly of death, but fear gave her the force of energy she needed. She gathered her senses and when she was sure both she and the baby were fine, she climbed up the tree again, this time careful to hang on. Once she settled in the safety of the enormous tree, Valentina took stock of her surroundings. At least up here she was fairly safe, and her fear subsided a bit. But it wasn't just fear of the dark and unfamiliar forest that scared her the most. What would happen when Antonio realized she wasn't home?

Chapter 13

Antonio strolled in the front door, expecting to find the pleasant smell of supper. But there was no smell, no supper, and no Valentina. Maybe she was playing one of her games, he decided. "Valentina?" he called, but there was no answer. He went to his mother's house, but she hadn't seen Valentina either.

"I did hear someone in the village say they thought they saw her running up the slope behind the house," she said, unable to keep the amusement out of her voice.

"You have to go find her. She must be frightened out there, all alone." Antonio's brother John stood up from the table. "I'll help you look for her," he offered.

"Let her find her own way back," Antonio snapped.

"What if this is some kind of test, and she's waiting to see if you'll come find her?" John countered. He was more than familiar with Antonio's treatment of his young wife.

"She should know better than to test me," Antonio growled at his brother.

"Fine. I'll go myself." John reached for his jacket and headed for the door.

Antonio was torn. He should teach her a lesson about leaving home when she was told not to. But after last night…

Shame over his actions spurred him to action. "Let's go."

It was twilight, but in an hour it would be impossible to search without lanterns. Antonio went home for his lantern, and met up with John at the edge of the forest. John lit his own lantern and together they ventured inside. Once they were far enough in, they started to call out for her. "Valentina!" they shouted over and over again as they moved deeper into the woods.

Valentina's eyes flew open. Did she hear a human voice through the frightening sounds of the forest? She raised her arm as if someone would be able to see it as she answered, "Over here!" But who had come to find her? Was she in danger of feeling Antonio's wrath once more? "Maybe it would be better to stay here," she muttered as she scanned the forest for her rescuers.

John found her first. She'd climbed into a tree and sat on a thick branch to protect her from the many creatures that roamed the forest floor. He put his lantern down on the ground and helped Valentina down. He reached under her arms and she felt secure as she jumped down. It was then that she noticed Antonio had reached them. "I'm sorry," she apologized quickly. "I was watching the sun, but somehow I lost my way, even though I tried to retrace my steps. I seemed to be going around in circles," she nervously explained.

Antonio didn't look like he believed her. He stood stiffly, legs spread apart, one hand on his hip and the other still clutching his lantern. "I can't believe you're still playing your stupid girl games. I don't give a damn how you lost your way. I'll break every one of your bones, and maybe that will keep you home doing your wifely duties."

He raised his hand to strike her. John's intervention wasn't quick enough. Antonio, relentless in his attack, caught a fistful of Valentina's hair as he barked out, "How many times am I going to tell you that I better not catch you with your hair unbound?"

Valentina gritted her teeth in pain as she said, "My hair is none of your concern."

With John between them, Antonio took a closer, threatening step. Furious, Valentina's anger gave strength to her words. "It was one thing that I should come here and endure your brute force and cruelty, but it is another thing to have you beat and abuse me in front of others. I have done everything in my power to do what is right in God's eyes."

John took pity on Valentina and said, "It's getting dark and we need to get going."

Antonio scowled at her, making Valentina feel embarrassed as well as afraid. Couldn't he see the worry in her eyes and notice the way she trembled? Any decent husband would have comforted and soothed his wife. Appalled and frustrated by his lack of reaction, she cried out, "I'll try not to disappoint you in the future!" She glanced at John, who seemed to understand her dilemma. He looked like he wanted to argue with Antonio, but chose to remain neutral.

"We have wasted enough time here, Antonio. She's all right and that's all that should matter. It's time to take your wife home." He picked up his lantern and started back the way they'd come.

Antonio turned his full attention on his nuisance of a wife. "Do you understand that not only did you put yourself in danger, but John and me as well?"

Valentina's voice was devoid of emotion as she replied, "I understand." It was bad enough she was embarrassed and sorry for putting him through this. Only time would heal her wounded heart, it seemed.

But he wasn't finished yet. "You have to grow up and act like a woman. I've had enough of your foolishness. Your precious guitar is firewood when we get home. Maybe that will teach you not to disobey me. I don't want to be reminded of your past anymore, Valentina."

Valentina knew she was taking a big chance, but she had to risk it. "In the future I'll try not to disappoint you. Please don't take away my guitar. I'll do anything you ask of me. You took me away from my family and friends but please don't take my guitar away from me!" she pleaded.

"You have me," he snapped at her.

"If you wouldn't leave me like a caged animal with your mother, I could go explore *Furnas*, make friends, breathe in the fresh air," she reasoned.

John had returned when they did not follow him. He heard Valentina's plea to his stubborn brother, and felt the need to step in. "She's right, Antonio," he said. "You can't blame your wife for the way men stare at her. You have a beautiful wife in case you hadn't noticed. She looks out of place because she's different, but she could shine here. You've been given a gift. Treasure it."

Antonio felt defeated by his brother's words. "I'll think about you staying home and running the house without my mother," he said slowly. "I'll give you some independence. But you have to curb your impulsiveness. I don't want you to run away and go back to *Arrifes* to your mother and sister." His voice had lost its sharpness. Suddenly he was too tired to fight her anymore.

Valentina felt like he'd given her a magical gift. It was more than she had hoped to get from him. She surprised herself as well as him by saying, "Now you have me." She closed the distance between them and kissed him. "I'm going to make the best of our marriage and the circumstances around it. I promise," she whispered in his ear.

* * *

Later that night, as thunder rumbled across the sky, Valentina willingly gave herself to her husband, and she allowed herself to fall asleep in his arms, her lips pressed against his neck. This was where she belonged. *I have to make this work,* she finally understood as she drifted off to sleep. Her life with Dimitri had to remain only a dream now. She had her future here, with Antonio and her baby. With time and patience she believed Antonio would come around and give her more freedom. At least this was a start.

* * *

Antonio opened his eyes and looked at his sleeping wife. Somehow they'd come to a fragile truce. He held on to the hope that she would some day love him. He knew he would have to be more open to her requests and not keep such a tight rein on her. It wasn't going to be easy, and truth be told it went against everything he believed about marriage, but he would at least try. He closed his eyes and snuggled closer to Valentina, sleep finally overtaking him.

Chapter 14

The next few weeks passed with little incident. Valentina and Antonio fell into a comfortable routine that allowed her enough freedom while he was still able to keep a watchful eye on her. The village women also began to warm up to Valentina, coming by to see her and including her in some of their community activities. Valentina now found herself baking and sewing, not just for her family, but also to contribute to the village. And all the while the baby constantly reminded her what all her hard work was for. At five months, Valentina was getting quite large, and she felt the baby move more frequently. It was a happier time for her, the strain of the early days of her marriage part of the past.

One day she sat outside, the sun shining down as she shucked corn for supper. A noise from the back of the house startled her, and thinking it was a hungry animal from the forest, she reached for the broom she kept nearby and prepared for the attack.

Gabriela emerged and laughed. "Were you planning to use that on me?" she teased.

Valentina let the broom drop and stood to hug her friend. "How did you manage to get away?" she asked. If Gabriela's husband found her here, they would both be in a lot of trouble.

"Ernesto is in *Povoação* today. He's trying to sell one of our pigs," she explained. "Money is a little tight right now, and he thought it was best."

Valentina could tell by her tone that Gabriela did not share her husband's opinion. "I'm sorry things are not going well for you right now," she said quietly.

"Nothing to worry over, believe me. We've been in worse spots before." It was well known that Ernesto Ponte was a heavy gambler, and not a very good one. "I came to ask you a favor," Gabriela said, quickly changing the subject. "My brother-in-law wants to meet you."

"I can't," Valentina replied quickly. Antonio would kill her if she went to meet a man behind his back. "Why?" she asked.

"He's heard of your singing, and he'd like to hire you to sing at the festival of St. Theresa next week. I told him I would ask you. He wanted to come himself, but I didn't think it was wise when Antonio wasn't home," Gabriela explained.

"A real job," Valentina said dreamily, and the baby fluttered in agreement. What would it be like to sing in front of a crowd again? she wondered. It had been so long, and she missed it so much. But would Antonio approve? "I'll have to ask my husband," she replied sadly. She already suspected what his answer would be.

* * *

"Absolutely not! Whatever made you think of something so ridiculous?" Antonio managed between mouthfuls of food. They sat together at the supper table. Valentina was so nervous that she could barely eat. Antonio did not seem to notice as he nearly inhaled his supper and drowned several mugs of wine in rapid succession. "Who is this man who wants to hire you?" he demanded.

"Augusto Ponte," Valentina replied. Her stomach was churning. This was not going well at all.

"That nut? He thinks he's some kind of town protector with all his fancy law talk and handouts. He borrows from one to help another. Nobody knows where the money comes from or where it goes. And if you're in trouble with the law, he always manages to clear you. Very convenient for someone who supposedly can't even spell his own name," Antonio mocked.

"He offered to pay well for a few hours of singing. That's all." Valentina tried to appeal to Antonio's sense of greed. If anything would make him come around, money would.

The mention of payment and the effects of the wine were taking a toll on Antonio. "How much?" he asked, calmer now.

"Enough to pay our rent through the winter," Valentina promised.

"I'll meet with him tomorrow and see what his terms are. I'll decide if it will be worth it." Antonio rose unsteadily to his feet and trudged up the stairs to the loft. "Don't keep me waiting," he called out.

"I won't." If this was what it took to sing again, Valentina thought as she hastily cleared away the remnants of supper, then she would gladly give herself over to Antonio. She climbed the stairs and readied for bed, her mind already on which songs she would sing at the festival.

* * *

"I think I'm being more than fair," Augusto Ponte offered as he sipped the tea Valentina had placed in front of him.

Across from him Antonio glared at their guest, his words measured and laced with barely suppressed anger. "My wife will sing if I say she will. You do not need her approval for any of this. You need mine."

"I'm afraid that's where you're wrong, Mr. Fero. Mrs. Fero

must agree to my terms, not you. I think the payment is more than generous, and I have been quite patient with you. Either she decides or the deal is off." Augusto Ponte continued to sip his tea slowly, unmoved by Antonio's harsh attitude.

Valentina did not know why, but she had taken an instant liking to him. His easygoing manner was so at odds with the other people she had met in the village. He had arrived at their door early in the afternoon, a ready smile on his lips. "Augusto Ponte at your service," he'd said. He'd taken her hand and shaken it, much to the chagrin of her husband. His grip was firm and confident. Valentina was struck by his keen, purposeful manner, as if he might have already solved her dilemma before Antonio had had a chance to pounce on the unsuspecting man. The fact that he had immediately stood up to her husband was admirable, indeed.

Antonio's defense seemed to crumble. He turned to Valentina and asked sarcastically, "Do you wish to sing at the festival?"

"Yes," she replied without hesitation. It was her chance to truly be independent, and she would not lose it.

"Very well then. That wasn't so hard after all, was it Mr. Fero?" Augusto Ponte did not give him a chance to reply. He shook Valentina's hand again and said, "I will see you Sunday afternoon in the village square. Good day, Mrs. Fero." He reached for the front door and stepped out into the sunshine.

"Can you believe the nerve of that bastard!" Antonio shoved away from the table and stood. "I will not be made a fool of in my own home! We'll see what happens on Sunday," he muttered as he grabbed his hat and left for the fields.

Valentina was crushed. Her brief chance at freedom was over in an instant. Antonio's pride wouldn't allow her to sing at the festival. There was only one thing she could do. She waited a few minutes to make certain Antonio wouldn't return home. She then pulled on her shawl and headed for Gabriela's. She was now more than familiar with the way there. Gabriela had walked her through which paths to take, and she navigated the forest like a seasoned explorer. Valentina had to tell her friend of Antonio's plan. She would not miss this once in a lifetime opportunity for anything in the world.

* * *

The day of the festival dawned rather cloudy, but by noon the sun blazed in the sky. Valentina dressed carefully, under the pretext that she was off to church. But Antonio was suspicious of her motives and declared that they would not attend mass today. Heartbroken, Valentina sat on her bench and tried not to cry as the clock inched its way to one, the time the festival was to start.

A sudden knock at the door brought her to her feet. Antonio reached the door first and pulled it open. "What do you want?" he growled.

Augusto Ponte stood on the threshold with two elderly women from the village. "We are here to accompany your wife. The festival starts in a few minutes," he answered evenly.

"She's not going," Antonio countered.

"I do believe I have a verbal agreement with you," he replied.

Valentina straightened her skirt and picked up her guitar as she reached the front door. "I'm ready," she said. She glanced at Antonio and asked sweetly, "Are you coming with us?"

"I wouldn't be caught dead at that damn festival." Antonio stepped back from the door and allowed her to pass. She was about to turn around and say good-bye when he slammed it shut in her face.

"Pay him no mind, Mrs. Fero. He's just sulking because I wouldn't let him intimidate me." Augusto offered to carry her guitar and the four of them walked in the direction of the *Parque de Beatrice*. "It was very wise of you to tell Gabriela of his plan. Otherwise I might not have known to come today," he added.

"Thank you for coming, Mr. Ponte," Valentina said. "I thought I would have to miss the festival," she admitted.

"No thanks are necessary. We had an agreement, and I chose to protect my investment, you could say." He smiled as he continued. "Your husband has never liked me. He thinks I'm a little crazy, and perhaps he's right. But I would not let him ruin this day for you."

They came into the heart of the village, straight to the town square. Valentina noted with satisfaction her mother-in-law's horrified expression as Augusto handed her the guitar. Valentina had no doubt that Antonio's mother suspected her daughter-in-law would be trapped at home today. "*Bom dia, minha sogra*," she said as she kissed the older woman on both cheeks.

Antonio's mother said nothing and turned away before Valentina could say anything else. So much for politeness, she reasoned as the crowd began to grow in anticipation of the concert that was about to start. She strategically sat on a thick wooden bench in the center of the square. From this vantage point she could see that the entire village had turned out for the festival. Antonio's brother John was there with several of his friends. Most of her brothers and sisters-in-law were there as well. She also spied Gabriela and her husband on the edge of the crowd. She quickly looked away as Ernesto Ponte gazed her way. She did not want him to know that she knew Gabriela, or it would mean trouble for her friend later. Valentina took a deep breath, prayed to God for a good performance, then picked up her guitar and began to sing: "*O minha mãe, minha mãe/ o minha mãe, minda amada/ quem tem uma mãe, tem todo/ quem não tem mãe, não tem nada.*"

The crowd responded well to her playing. Groups of people began to sing along with her, and some even ran home to retrieve their own instruments to join in the concert. Augusto Ponte took his turn at a few songs, alternatively singing and playing his own guitar with Valentina on several Azorean favorites. She almost missed a chord as she watched Antonio make his way through the crowd and sit not too far from her. He appeared relaxed, but she noticed his watchful eyes scanning the crowd around her, and more than once he shot Augusto Ponte a dirty look. If anyone noticed her sudden distress, they either ignored it or did not care. The crowd was worked up into a near frenzy, with both children and adults dancing and singing long into the night.

It was nearly one in the morning when Augusto called a halt to the festival and thanked everyone for coming before sending them all home to sleep. Tomorrow was a workday, after all.

"Mrs. Fero," Augusto called out as she started back towards home. Antonio was nowhere in sight; it looked as if she would be walking home alone. "I have your money for you," he reminded her as she slung her guitar over her shoulder and scanned the dissipating crowd one last time.

"Thank you," she replied, distracted. Antonio started towards her from the shadows, his stride purposeful. At first she thought she was in trouble for sure, but he surprised her by pulling a small bouquet of wildflowers from behind his back and placing a kiss on her forehead.

"You sang like a hummingbird," he muttered. He did not bother to acknowledge Augusto, but added as he gently took her hand, "Let's go home."

"Well, I see you won't need me to take you home then. Good night Mrs. Fero and thank you." He tipped his cap at her and strolled away.

Wordlessly Antonio led her to the waiting cart. He helped her up, then pulled a blanket from the back and draped it across her shoulders. He hopped up into his seat and snapped the reins. "Did you have a good time?" he asked as they slowly rumbled towards home.

"I did, very much." What a day it had been! The adoration of the crowd, the joyous singing and dancing that accompanied every song, and the applause…it was everything she had missed for so long. She could not have been happier if a million *escudos* suddenly fell from the sky. "Why did you come?" she asked, instantly fearful. Was he still angry? Would he beat her for holding to her agreement with Augusto Ponte?

"I missed your voice," he said after a long moment. "I only wanted to hear you sing."

He rolled to a stop in front of the house and helped her down. "You should get to bed," he said quietly. "It's been a long day and you must be tired."

"But supper," she began.

"I'm not hungry," he interrupted. "Good night Valentina." He kissed her cheek and opened the front door for her, then turned back to put the donkey and cart away.

Valentina studied him a moment as he worked in the cool, moonlit yard. His profile cut a strong line through the darkness, and she smiled in spite of herself. She clutched her flowers in one hand and wondered what had made Antonio so understanding this evening. Whatever it was, she silently prayed, please let it last. She entered the house and readied herself for bed.

Antonio let out a ragged sigh as she shut the door, his mind in turmoil. He knew he had every right to be angry with her for going to the festival, but the truth was that he really had missed her singing. She had not been happy for a long time, and he knew that he was to blame for a lot of that. He unhitched the cart from the donkey and led the animal to the barn. He would let her sing more often, if that would make their home life a little more pleasant. But it would be on his terms, not Augusto Ponte's. They had never been friends, and he'd be damned if they were going to start now.

A blast of cold air made him shiver as he shut the barn door and returned for the cart. He suddenly felt the need to get inside and climb into the warmth and safety of his bed, though he didn't know why. Antonio quickly finished the last of his chores and headed for bed, an unsettled feeling lulling him into a restless sleep.

Chapter 15

Valentina walked out to the bean path in the back yard carrying an empty bowl that she would use to fill up with beans for supper. She sat down on the thick, fresh grass with the bowl in her lap, and let her thoughts drift. The situation with Antonio had improved somewhat, but she still felt trapped in this place, among these people who tried to accept her but kept a wall between them for protection. She felt cheated, even though she was now able to sing in the village square on Sundays, and Antonio did not watch her as closely as he once did. Even her mother-in-law had found other things to fill her day besides spying on her wayward daughter-in-law all the time. But there was one thing that still nagged at her, and she could not allow the matter to rest. "Why was I born poor?" she whispered into the small garden. The plants and trees offered no response, but she had one other question she needed to clear from her conscience. "Why am I still daydreaming about Dimitri?" A tear rolled down her cheek as she allowed herself to think of him. "I had no business falling in love with a rich boy, knowing nothing could ever come of it." Thinking of it aloud, Valentina was filled with hurt and anger. If their destinies had been decided, then why had they fallen in love? Nature had played a mean trick. With the joining of their bodies, there had been no question of guilt, right or wrong. "It was the consummation of our love," she spoke softly as memories assailed her. She remembered how he'd tenderly held her. "Is he missing me as much as I miss him?" she asked bitterly. She choked back her sobs as she considered how differently her life had turned out. "Who laid the law edicts of marriage?" she demanded of her surroundings as she replayed the quiet but uneventful life she had resigned herself to. It wasn't fair to blame anyone but herself. She had chosen, and her choice had been motivated by need, not love. *And this is what I must accept,* she thought sadly as she rose to pick the beans for supper.

* * *

Dimitri lingered in the orchard, haunted by old memories. Had it been only a few months since Valentina walked out of his life forever? "Why did she let herself get talked into that marriage," he wondered of the heavens, "when she's in love with me?" His eyes stung with the memory of that love. At times, he thought he would lose his mind. He felt so helpless. Dimitri had an emptiness in his heart he knew no other woman could ever fill. "I'll never marry anyone else," he vowed. The thought of sharing his life, his bed, and his future with any other woman left a hollow, cold void in his chest. He would emerge from this dark tunnel and dedicate himself to that which he was born to, like his father had. Everyone in the village had either a stone house with dirt floors or simple straw huts. His father's house was far grander than any of those, constructed of brick and granite, a monument to his success.

"If I cannot love Valentina, I will love my work and enjoy my success," he decided. But he could not do it here, not where she had walked and loved with him, where everywhere he had memories of her. He would travel to America and study there, and become a great doctor, better than his father, better than anyone in this tiny, poor village. It was a selfish thought, but Fate had been cruel and unforgiving so far in his life. He would channel that anger and achieve through his life's purpose what he could not have in love. Saddened by the path his thoughts traveled, Dimitri walked towards home, Valentina's torn and dirty apron clutched in one hand. He had found it under a tree earlier that day, still wrapped around some rotted oranges. It had seen far better days, and was more suited to the rag pile, but it was his only link to her. He carefully tucked it under his arm and walked away from the orchard for the last time.

* * *

Valentina went into the forest the same time every day. She suspected Antonio knew what she was up to, but he said nothing. There she found Gabriela already lying on the grass. Valentina always brought her guitar wrapped in her shawl and played for her friend. She would sing for Gabriela, and in exchange Gabriela had offered to teach her to read and write. She brought a small stone tablet with her and carefully scratched words and letters onto its smooth surface with a piece of old chalk.

Sitting with her legs folded under her, elbows on her knees, Valentina took one look at Gabriela's kind brown eyes and knew she could trust her friend with the biggest secret of her life. She took a deep breath and confessed everything to Gabriela. "Antonio is not the father of my baby," she admitted as tears poured down her face. "I was in love with another man in my village, and we had planned to be married when I found out I carried his baby. But I would never have been allowed to marry Dimitri. His family is very wealthy and his mother was very clear that I would be in serious trouble if I pushed the issue. I knew my baby would need a father, or I would be cast out of my village.

I married Antonio even though my closest friend was in love with him because he tried to court me and I knew I could have some kind of life with him as my husband."

She drew in a shaky breath as a huge burden lifted from her shoulders. Valentina went on to tell her that she had felt the baby kick for the first time and she couldn't bring herself to share it with Antonio. "It should be Dimitri putting his hand on my stomach and feeling the first ripple of movement from the baby," she further confided. "Antonio knows the baby is not his. He married me anyway, out of some sense of pride and male honor. I think he felt he'd won some contest, like I was a prize he had to steal away from another man. I've accepted my marriage and all of the ups and downs that have come with it. But my heart will always belong to Dimitri."

Valentina shook her head sadly. "Why does life have to be so complicated, Gabriela? I would have been so happy with Dimitri. We would have shared a wonderful life together."

Taking her friend's hand in her own, Gabriela smiled gently and said, "I wish I had the answers to those questions, Valentina. It could help me explain my own life. But I will take your secret to my grave. You have nothing to fear. But you must try to make the best of your life. You have to close your eyes and pretend everything is as you want it to be. That is what I do when I am sad. Here we have freedom," she said as her eyes scanned the surrounding forest. "We don't need to feel like lepers. We don't need to pretend with each other to everyone around us. They think everything we do is tinged with imperfection. But we're unique, free to think and feel the way we want, and we should be proud of the women we have become. No one can take that away from us."

Valentina dropped her eyes and answered quietly, "Look at me. I'm eighteen and I'm going to have a baby. I do not belong with Antonio, but with Dimitri. I wish I could repeat my seventeenth year, where I was happy, and with Dimitri. Growing up is so hard," Valentina lamented as she stared at the water spilling from the stone wall.

Gabriela did not want to see her friend so distressed. Smiling, she reached for Valentina's guitar and handed it to her, saying, "Here, sing me a song."

She sat with her knees pulled up to her chest as Valentina strummed the guitar, tears streaming down her face as she sang her favorite song: "Forbidden to love you/ forbidden to call your name/ to Christ I tell of my sorrow/ and he responds to me/ rest my love for I will comfort you."

When Valentina finished her song, she sat motionless, sadness overwhelming her. With her thumb she absently stuck the same chord repeatedly. Gabriela reached for her and in spite of her tears, Valentina laughed. Wordlessly Gabriela wrapped her arm around Valentina and she curled into her friend's comforting embrace. Weeping, she managed to say, "Now that my belly is full, I'm no longer attractive to my husband. Whatever he might have felt for me before, he can't even manage that much now. He doesn't look at me the same way. Even that I'm denied."

Gabriela chuckled as she continued to hug her. "I think you have more important things to worry about than what Antonio thinks of your big belly, like the life that's inside it."

Valentina laughed, her tears slowing as she straightened up and dried her eyes. "I know," she replied as she stood and reached for her guitar. "What a sorry sight I am today."

They both continued to laugh as Gabriela decided to walk Valentina home. Ernesto was away again, selling another pig. She knew that he took the money and spent it on other women, but Gabriela did not share this with Valentina. The poor girl had more than enough to deal with. She would not add to her burdens. They picked their way across the now well-worn path and started back.

*   *   *

That evening Valentina was not feeling well. She was pale, fatigued, and vomiting, so she went to bed early. Antonio did not make a fuss, surprisingly. He declared he was going to have a smoke with the men who were playing cards down the road at the tavern, and left soon afterward. It had been a long day anyway, and Valentina was glad for the brief reprieve from her wifely duties. As she started to drift off to sleep, a thought suddenly occurred to her, something her mother had always said as she was growing up: *Someday you're going to grow up, and if you're ever touched by love, that love multiplies just as you give it.* But how could that be right, Valentina wondered, since she and Dimitri could not be together? Closing her eyes and burying her face in her pillow, she cried her heart out. "Dimitri," she whispered into the empty room, "you are the one I want to cry with, laugh with, and love."

A while later Valentina heard faint footsteps approach. She heard Antonio undress, and finally his side of the mattress sagged. He blew out the lantern and lay on his side with his back to her. She listened as he snored lightly, which made her cry silently. She thought he might touch her shoulder and ask if she was all right. Valentina cradled her distended abdomen and thoughts of Dimitri persisted. Her love for him refused to wither. With every passing day, there was a growing feeling of detachment from Antonio, which only increased her loneliness.

*   *   *

The village midwife now came on a regular basis. Her impending delivery brought her restless nights. Her face and lips got puffy and her ankles swelled to the point where she could only walk a few steps at a time. The midwife told Valentina that her lethargy was normal and would pass with the birth of the baby. She was the only kind person in Valentina's life, with the exception of Gabriela, that responded to her. Valentina's days brightened considerably when she received word from her mother and sister. The letters that she had hoped for had not come for some time, but when they finally started, she received them regularly. And now she was able to respond to them, thanks to Gabriela's patient and careful tutoring. But this letter was different, Valentina realized as she tore open the envelope.

"I have good news," her mother began. "Your sister and I are going to America. Because your sister was born there, she's a citizen of that great country. We are going in search of a better life. We will be able to send you clothes and food, and some day you and your family can travel to America. The few months since you left feel like so many. We miss you, and best of luck with the baby. Love, your mother."

Feeling a mixture of emotions, from happiness for her family's improved life change, but sadness over knowing her mother would no longer be only a few villages away, Valentina folded the letter and placed it in her apron pocket. Now her mother and sister would be crossing an ocean as big as the sky. This separation was not going to be easy. It was so final. Valentina tried not to dwell on it anymore as she set out the supper dishes. She wanted her family to be happy. At least they had a way out, while she did not.

That night after supper Antonio noticed that Valentina looked very sad. She saw the questioning look on his face and told him of the letter. "My family is going to America," she explained as tears threatened to spill forth.

She expected reassurance or at least an expression of concern, but his face was void of any emotion. The tears she had not cried since reading the letter now ran freely down her cheeks. How could he be so cold, so uncaring?

Somewhere inside Antonio a battle raged. Quiet hung over them both for a long while, but he managed to find some compassion for her and reached out. They shared an awkward embrace, and he pulled back slightly to wipe at her tears with his thumb. He closed his eyes and smelled her hair, his thoughts chaotic. He did love her, more than she would ever probably believe. But the reminder of her ever-increasing belly pressed against him, and knowing that it was not his child she carried, weighed heavily. He wanted to show her some compassion, some measure of understanding, but pride warred with his heart.

They accidentally bumped noses and he captured her lips with a kiss as they laughed together. He risked a brief, intimate caress. He moved his hand to cup her breast, and lower to her extended belly. Valentina wanted to encourage him. She covered one of his hands and said, "It's all right. You can't hurt the baby." She felt Antonio tense. "Don't pull away, Antonio. Please don't reject me. You're all I have," she pleaded.

But Antonio pulled back. He suddenly seemed very far away. "I'm sorry," he said, "I just can't."

Desperately Valentina reached out to him again. "Please, Antonio, accept this baby as yours. No one knows but you and me who the baby's father is. *Our* baby, Antonio," she whispered.

He wanted to say something to her that would erase the pain and anguish on her face, but he couldn't. Without a word he pulled away from her again and left the house and Valentina for his usual walk down to the tavern to drink his problems away. "I wish I could be more for you," he whispered into the night air. The wind howled through the trees in answer, a lonely and mournful wail that echoed his broken and battered heart.

Valentina stood silent, her eyes glued to the front door. *Please come back*, she begged, but in her heart she knew he couldn't do that. Her baby would always come between them. There was nothing else she could do. She cleared away supper and readied for bed, knowing he would not be home until very late, and until he had managed to block out his troubles with enough strong wine to make coming home easier.

Chapter 16

"There's a salesman in the village who just came from *Arrifes.*" Valentina's brother-in-law John carried the bucket over to the pen and dumped the scraps in. As the pigs raced to their lunch, he added, "Maybe he has some news for you."

Valentina looked up from her sewing and replied, "How can I go and ask when I can't even use the outhouse without someone knowing about it? Your mother still watches me like a hawk, even thought Antonio told her to stop. She's always trying to catch me doing something I'm not supposed to. I feel like a prisoner here. I can't even go into the village to buy cheese without hearing a detailed account of it later."

The situation with Antonio had improved a great deal, but there were still some things they had not compromised on. She was not allowed into the village without a very good reason. And though her mother-in-law had relaxed her guard-like status, every once in a while she liked to see what Valentina was up to, and made sure to let Antonio know. Whether she was innocent or not, Valentina found it was too much trouble to constantly have to defend herself against her daily routine. So she elected to stay home as much as possible, except to see Gabriela. Her enormous belly also made long walks more difficult these days, so it was better to stay home and away from gossiping tongues.

John came to sit next to her. "He's working his way, village by village. I think he'll pass this way tomorrow morning. Talk to him then." John looked down at his hands, his expression thoughtful. "You're not the only one who's watched around here. But I'll try to keep my mother busy so you can have a chance to ask him about your family."

"Thank you John." Valentina studied her brother-in-law as she continued to sew. John was not like the other Fero men. Though he matched them in looks, his personality was very different. He was Antonio's total opposite. John had a softer, philosophical air about him. While the others settled their disputes with their fists, John chose reason and compromise. Dozens of girls hoped he might choose a wife soon. But John was strangely silent about wanting a relationship. His brothers would often go into the village to drink, but he would always stay behind, preferring his own company instead of the attention of the village girls. Valentina suspected there was more to his reluctance than he said, and she decided to call him on it.

"John?" she called out. He looked up and smiled. "Why don't you settle down and find a nice girl to marry?" she asked.

John's face fell. He ran a hand through his hair and tried not to look at her. "It's complicated," he answered.

"Why? Don't any of the girls appeal to you? What about Mrs. Pereira's daughter? She's very pretty," Valentina tried.

John took a while to answer. "No Valentina, none of them appeal to me." He stood up and paced the yard, his hands clasped behind his back. "I don't feel comfortable with women," he explained. He stopped and looked at Valentina, his eyes filled with tears. "I'm not like other men."

Valentina stared at him, confused. If he didn't care for women, then what…understanding struck her. "So you would prefer a relationship with a…"

"With a man," he finished. "Now you see my dilemma."

"I suppose I do," Valentina admitted. "Does your family know?" she asked.

"No! And they never can, Valentina. My father would skin me alive if he knew." John again sat next to her. "His name is Miguel."

"The baker's son?" Valentina's eyes went wide with surprise.

"Yes. He makes me very happy." John smiled at her. "Are you shocked?" he asked.

"A little. But I'm glad you're happy. And I promise I'll take your secret to my grave." Valentina shook her head. She always thought John was a little different, but she never imagined this. He was the only one of the Fero relatives who genuinely cared about her and had no hidden motives when he helped her or talked to her. She found she could confide in him much like she could with Gabriela. He was the brother she'd never had. But he was right. His family would never understand. She knew all too well about loving someone everyone else thought was wrong for you.

"Thank you." He gave her a quick hug and stood. "I told him I'd visit tonight. I should leave before it gets too dark. I'll see you tomorrow, Valentina." John started across the yard.

"Until tomorrow." Valentina resumed her sewing. Even John was happier than she was. She glanced down at her enormous belly, an unconscious gesture that reminded her of what this was all for.

* * *

Valentina scanned the yard, her nerves rattled. Antonio's mother had breezed through the kitchen that morning, announced she had to work in the fields because John was ill, and told her to have supper ready for everyone tonight. "Thank you

John," Valentina whispered as she watched her mother-in-law march across the yard and climb into her cart. She rattled off, leaving Valentina free to do what she wanted for the day. She prayed the salesman from *Arrifes* would come by. If John was right, maybe he could tell her if her family had left for America yet, and whether Ana was still in *Arrifes*. But most of all, she wanted to hear about Dimitri.

The hours dragged on as she tried to find things to do. She cleaned the kitchen, made herself some lunch, folded the clean laundry, and then peeled the vegetables for supper, all the while staring out the window in hopes of glimpsing the salesman.

It was well after noon when he walked up to the door and prepared to knock. But Valentina flung it open and ushered him inside before anyone could see him. "Please sit down," she said as she poured him a mug of milk and set out some biscuits.

"Thank you. John asked me to come by here. He said you hoped for news of your family." He took a bite from a biscuit and sat back. "You're Maria Marques' daughter. I remember you as a child."

"Yes. Have you any news of her?" she asked eagerly.

The man thought for a moment. "She's well," he finally said. "She boarded a ship with your sister for America a week ago. I think they are headed for a place called New York."

"I see." So her mother had followed her dream of a better life and set out for America. She was happy for them, but a little sad for her own sorry state. She would probably never see them again, nor would she see herself free of the poverty and misery that had plagued her since birth. "And what of Ana Silveira?" she asked after a moment.

"She married a nice young man from *Agua de Peixo*. His family owns a lot of land." He gulped down his milk. "You married John's brother Antonio, didn't you?"

"I did. We're expecting a baby very soon." It was a small lie, but this stranger could not suspect why she would ask him her next question. "What about the Maciel family?" Her heart thudded against her ribs as she waited for his answer.

"Their son took off to Lisbon, I think. Medical school or some such nonsense. His parents still live in *Arrifes*." He stood and walked over to the front door. "Thank you for your hospitality, and congratulations on your baby." He opened the door. "I need to get going if I want to reach the next village by sunset and visit the rest of the homes in the area."

"Good-bye, and thank you," Valentina called out as he crossed the yard to the road beyond. She had been so engrossed in what he was saying that she had forgotten to ask his name. "Thank you," she called softly. At least she now had some idea of how Dimitri faired. He had left for school just as his mother predicted. *And he went to marry his betrothed,* she thought sadly.

She cleaned up the table, removing any trace of a visitor in the house. She rinsed the empty mug and put it away. She'd found out what she needed to. Ana had found the husband she'd longed for, and her family was headed for a better life in a new home. And Dimitri...She tried not to let the ache in her heart bother her as she set about preparing the rest of supper. She wanted him to be happy, and she knew that could not happen if they were together. "I'm sorry, Dimitri," she said as she touched her belly. She had made her choice, and now it was too late. Dimitri was gone, for good.

* * *

Antonio's mother spurred the horse on, her mind on a nice, warm supper and a good night's sleep. The work in the fields today had been slow and tedious. She rounded the corner and pulled into her yard. A man stood at her door, knocking to see if anyone was home. "Who's there?" she called out as she climbed down from the cart.

The man walked over to her and extended his hand. "*Boa tarde, Senhora.* I am going village to village, selling household goods. I wonder if you might have a few minutes to spare?"

"Of course." Mrs. Fero loved new things. She ushered the man inside and asked him to sit down. "Where have you come from?" she asked as she set out a plate of *massa* and some milk.

"*Arrifes*," he replied through mouthfuls of the delicious sweet bread.

"My daughter-in-law is from there," she said conversationally. *And I wish she'd go back*, she added silently.

"Then you must mean Valentina Fero," he supplied. "I spoke with her not too long ago."

"Really?" This was interesting news. Won't Antonio love hearing about this! "Did she ask you about her family?" she questioned, her curiosity aroused.

"Yes she did." The man drained his mug and smiled. "May I have some more?" he asked.

Antonio's mother refilled the mug and sat across from him. "Well, what did you tell her?" she demanded.

He looked at her strangely, but replied, "Her mother and sister just left for America, and a friend of hers just married. Oh, and she asked about the Maciels," he added.

"The Maciels?" Antonio's mother had never heard of these people. "I don't think I know them," she replied vaguely.

"Dr. Maciel is the village physician. His son Dimitri just left for Lisbon to study medicine as well. It was rumored that he and Valentina were to be married, and then she suddenly married your son. But you knew all of that," he said.

"Of course," Mrs. Fero answered a little too quickly. She did some rapid calculations. Antonio had been married for five months, and the baby was almost due. He had not been in Arrifes that long when he married Valentina. An evil grin spread across her face as she realized the true connection between Valentina and this Dimitri Maciel.

The salesman felt the room grow cold and hastily excused himself. "I really must be going," he stammered.

"But what about your wares?" she asked.

"Another time, Mrs. Fero. I really need to go." He rose quickly and left.

"You little *puta*!" she thought to herself. "You've been passing that baby off as my son's all this time, but I'm on to your little game now." She reached for her shawl and headed for Antonio's house. She had a few things to say to her daughter-in-law.

Chapter 17

Valentina wanted to sit in the sun while she wrote her mother a letter. She laid out a straw mat in her front doorway. There she settled her guitar and her writing tablet. She had to squeeze onto the top step because it had gotten so crowded. As she prepared to write, a young man walking down the road called out, "*Bom dia*!"

Valentina looked up to reply when she noticed her mother-in-law coming her way, her face sagged with worry. Through her shawl Valentina could see her breasts bouncing from her hurried steps. She looked old and disheveled, and immediately Valentina asked what was wrong.

Clutching her skirt in one hand and a walking stick in the other, she replied breathlessly, "What's wrong? I'll tell you what's wrong!"

Valentina sensed big trouble ahead. She ushered the older woman into the house to avoid unwanted attention. Whatever the problem was, it had her in quite a state. Mrs. Fero rushed inside past Valentina and planted herself in the middle of the room, her intimidating stance causing Valentina to shrink back in fear.

Antonio's mother took one look at her daughter-in-law's belly and accused, "I know why you married my son! What kind of witch's potion have you given him to blind him so?"

Valentina's mouth fell open. What on earth was this woman talking about? She attempted to say something, but Mrs. Fero cut her off. Her face trembling with barely concealed rage, the old woman raised a closed fist into the air and wailed, "You don't carry Antonio's baby! Don't even try to deny it! I know your kind and all the arguments you're going to give me! You want me to accept this child of sin as my grandchild!" She lowered her hand and took a deep breath. "We are poor people, but we are honorable and respectable. None of my daughters has shamed me this way, and neither will you. You are nothing but a *puta*! I know all about how you came to embarrass my son and his family, and take away the shame from your own family. You didn't want to be shunned in your village, but you don't care if my family is shunned here."

Valentina stood speechless, her mind in a panic. How did Antonio's mother know? "*Minha sogra*," she tried again, "I'm sorry..."

Antonio's mother did not let her finish. "If my son lets you stay here, you are on your own. You will not have my support or the family's support. After today you are no longer our concern. Now get out of my way!" She shoved Valentina aside, slamming her into the wall, and stormed from the house. She lifted her shawl to her head and spoke her last words to her daughter-in-law without a backward glance: "Don't ever come looking for me again!"

Valentina watched her go, feeling an odd combination of fear and relief. At last the secret was no longer hers alone. She did not have to pretend that Antonio was the loving father that he could never be. But fear clawed at her heart. She didn't know what to do next. Did Antonio know that his mother knew? Did anyone else know? And how did she find out? Suddenly feeling like the sinner she was accused of being, she sat and waited for Antonio, hoping for answers. But Antonio did not come home for supper.

She waited a long while, hoping against hope that when he did return, they would be able to work out the situation before her mother-in-law had a chance to spread the word throughout the village. But the hours crept by and Antonio still did not come home. Exhausted, Valentina finally gave up and wearily climbed the stairs to the loft. A strange, wet sensation started between her legs, and she knew her water had broken. The midwife had prepared her for this, and robotically Valentina moved to the bed and sat motionless, her arms wrapped around her belly. She wondered at the future she would have with her baby as she waited for the pains the midwife had described to her. As Fate would have it, she had been born poor, while Dimitri had been born rich enough that his parents thought her beneath him. They would never have accepted this baby.

She stared into the darkness and remembered her mother's parting words. Life would have been so cruel had she stayed in her village, except that life here wasn't any better. She lay down, the first of her labor pains convulsing through her body. She waited for Antonio, and for the baby. They were her only sources of comfort now. Gently sliding her hands over her belly, she felt the form of a foot against the wall of her womb. The baby had run out of room. For the past two weeks she had not felt it rolling around in its liquid world. She wanted to wait up for Antonio, but her exhaustion turned to sleep. Her last thought was of Dimitri: *He should be here tonight with me.*

Valentina awoke to find Antonio standing by the bed. "I have a very difficult and painful decision to make," he informed her.

"Not now, Antonio, please. The baby is coming," she pleaded. "It's time."

But he did not seem to hear her. "I spoke with my mother today. All of my brothers and sisters know the baby isn't mine. I need time to think and evaluate what's best for my family and me."

Valentina tried to sit up as another contraction wracked her body. "Please forgive me," she cried out, although she wasn't even sure what she wanted him to forgive. "Please don't send me away." She reached up and touched his arm. If ever she needed comfort and understanding, this was the time.

Antonio looked down at her hand on his arm. He sighed and withdrew from her, turned around and left the room. But the seeds of guilt had been planted. He was torn by the voice of his conscience. "How am I supposed to forgive her," he wondered aloud as he settled himself in the front doorway, "when I'm the one who instilled all the mental insecurities within her?" The cool night air brushed over him, and Antonio allowed himself to feel all of the doubts and confusion that had plagued him since the day he'd decided to make Valentina his wife.

"I can't pretend I can deal with the challenges ahead." He did not know whom he addressed; he supposed God listened somewhere as he poured his heart out into the night. "I want to find true peace. I'm choking with the grief of the aggression and physical pain I've caused her. These tongue-wagging people would call the baby a bastard, but if I send her away, she'll be banished in shame."

It seemed there were no ready answers for him this night. He rose and entered the house again. From upstairs he heard Valentina scream out, "It's time! Go get the midwife!"

He froze at the bottom of the stairs. He wasn't ready for this, not yet. But he stirred himself to action before he lost his nerve, and ran from the house to get the midwife. The other news he had to share with Valentina would have to wait until later. His mother had taken to her bed, paralyzed from a sudden stroke she suffered a few hours before, after he had confessed about the baby. She had been unable to talk or move, and Antonio had taken one look at his mother and blamed Valentina. The whole situation had been too much for her to handle. But as he raced the cart down the narrow road, he had only himself to blame. Guilt and pride had kept him from telling the truth long ago. He did not know how his mother had found out, only that she had not been surprised when he had come to her with his news. And now her suffering could be added to his list of sins as well.

While Antonio went for the midwife, Valentina tried desperately not to cry out as the labor pains increased. With eyes wide open, she lay there alone, waiting them out. As the pains eased she ran her fingers through her hair in relief. She could make out voices coming near, and turned to see the midwife walking towards her, a lantern in one hand. Antonio had asked her how long the labor would take, and she replied that it could take a long time, especially with a first baby. She lifted the lantern high as if in search of something, and smiled when she saw Valentina's face. "Has your time come, *querida*?" she asked kindly.

Surprised by her kind words, Valentina struggled to find her voice as another wave of pain hit her. "Yes," she said simply. "My water broke and I've been having pains."

"Well," replied the midwife, "sometimes the first time is not easy. This night will turn into morning before the baby comes. Now let me have a look at you." She moved closer to Valentina and set the lantern aside. After examining her, she looked at Valentina and took her hand. "First babies can be stubborn," she explained, "and it's going to be awhile for this one. I will go home, and return at sunrise. Antonio will watch you through the night."

With each hour the pain worsened. Each contraction was longer than the last, and her belly was hard as stone. After Antonio had taken the midwife home, he'd returned and brought up a stool to sit by the bed, his elbows on his knees and his face in his hands. He had said very little the entire night, and as

Valentina experienced her next pain, tears sprang to her eyes. If Dimitri had been here, he would have been attentive to her. He would have held her hand and spoken encouraging words. But Antonio merely sat and stared at her as if he didn't even know her. She could feel the distance between them grow even as she knew she would need him now more than ever.

Valentina did not think the contractions could get any worse, but she was wrong, and the latest one left her gasping for air. Just as Antonio finally showed some signs of life and rose with nervousness, the front door opened and a familiar voice rose up to Valentina like music in her ears. "I'm here," announced the midwife.

Valentina twisted, turned, and moaned with the next contraction, and the midwife wiped her face with a cool cloth. "Oh my," Valentina panted as the pain shot through her. The midwife offered Valentina her hands to grip, then guided her to hold onto the headboard for support with the next one as the pain lessened.

"It won't be long now," the midwife reassured her. Within a few minutes the pains were so excruciating, with no relief between each one that Valentina literally lifted off the mattress. The final contraction struck so intensely that she gripped the headboard for dear life and with a loud moan, called out for Dimitri. She felt an instant relief as the baby slipped from her body into the world. "It's a boy," the midwife announced softly. She had mistaken Valentina's cry for the baby's name, and added, "It's little Dimitri."

Antonio's head shot up. Throughout the labor he had said nothing, unsure of what, if anything, he could do to help. For a few brief moments, he'd almost believed that the tiny life Valentina carried might in part belong to him. But the midwife's seemingly innocent comment twisted like a knife in his gut. He had no claim to this child, a fact made clear from the moment of his birth.

Through burning tears and still taking short breaths, Valentina looked down when she felt a wet, slippery form on her belly. The midwife took Valentina's hands and gently put them on the baby. "Hold him like this," she instructed, "while I cut the cord and tend to the afterbirth." She then washed the baby, wrapped him in a white flannel blanket and handed him to his smiling mother, though Valentina's tired features were distorted from the rigors of childbirth.

Valentina saw Dimitri in her newborn child. She felt the baby shiver and tucked him under her blanket, his tiny body held close to her bosom. The baby sought her breast with his hungry mouth, and with further instructions from the midwife, she fed her newborn son. Valentina bent her head and whispered, "I will call you my little blond prince." She smiled once more as she shifted him in her arms and listened to the squalls coming out of the baby's mouth.

Antonio came over to the bed, his eyes sad. Perhaps there was some hope, he thought as he took a look at Valentina and then finally at the baby. But he saw no other face there than Dimitri's. With an anguished roar, he cried out, "He's a bastard child!"

"Stop it, please! Don't hold any resentment towards the baby! He is innocent of any evil that I have done in your eyes!" Valentina pleaded through simmering tears, "He's our son. We have to embrace life with this new life. If you are open to it, it will be the substance of our marriage."

Antonio was beside himself. "What am I going to say to everyone when they see him? He's whiter than the sheet he's wrapped in! If you had given birth to an olive complexioned, brown-haired baby, maybe in time I could come to accept him." But this child bore no resemblance to him, and little to Valentina. No one would ever believe this was his son.

The baby began to cry with all the shouting, and the midwife took him from Valentina to try and soothe him. She thought that Valentina dressed much too old for her age, and looked far older than she actually was, but the trials of childbirth had aged her considerably. Most occasions turned out joyous, but there were those few, like now, she thought sadly, when the promise of new life was overshadowed by petty differences and the inability to see reason. She had seen it before, and knew that this same scene would be repeated many times over, many children later. She took compassion on Valentina, and driven by some maternal instinct, advanced toward Antonio and said, "She needs her rest. It is not the right time for this."

Antonio was about to protest when a voice called from the bottom of the stairs. Valentina was suddenly filled with hope—it was John. He asked for permission to come up to the loft and faced his brother. Grief tore through him at his mother's sudden illness, and he knew the cause. But he would not let Antonio bring further pain down on his family by hardening his heart against his wife and child, regardless of the baby's parentage. "It won't be necessary for you to send Valentina away," he said calmly. "I will take them both away from here and provide for them. I will take my share of the money and build a new life for us. The baby will not live in a place like this."

The midwife sensed the increased tension in the room and made a hasty retreat with the baby downstairs. "Dear mother of God," she whispered as she descended the stairs. It felt as if a war were about to erupt in the tiny loft above.

Antonio sneered at his brother, and casually remarked, "You mean live in a place like this as you have with your little secrets. What a pair you'll make! I'm sure you'll be the best of girlfriends."

Valentina screamed out, "You must stop this! Stop hurting each other!" She pleaded with her brother-in-law. "John, don't inflict this pain on yourself! Leave now, before you both regret it!"

Antonio laughed at her, his eyes cold. "Honesty tugs at my heart, John," he mocked. "Tell her John. Tell all of us about your secret." As John spoke up Antonio cut him off with a wave of his hand. "No, on second thought, let me." He turned to Valentina and said, "John is not interested in the opposite sex. So we all know it's not your beauty that has captivated him. It's your free spirit he envies. Wouldn't it be nice to let your hair down and pick up your skirts for a run through the fields John? Or would you prefer to sit by the hearth and sew with the other village women?"

Valentina took pity on John and called out, "You're an animal, Antonio! Why don't you just…" Valentina screamed as John punched her husband squarely in the nose. Antonio reeled back and nearly tumbled down the loft stairs as he vainly tried to stop the blood flowing from his face and hold on to the railing.

John stepped back, horrified at what he'd just done. He reached to help his brother but Antonio shook him off. Valentina's tears poured down her face as she cried, "Now see what you've done Antonio! Do you hold the waters of life in your hands?" she accused. When Antonio did not reply, she pushed on. "John has a right to hold on to his true self! Stop punishing all of us!" She squeezed her eyes shut as she tried to block out Antonio's venomous words, but they replayed in her mind again and again.

John leaned over and kissed the top of her head. "I'm sorry," he whispered. He descended the stairs and fled the house.

Antonio took a look at her and felt a pang of regret. He started to reach for her, then thought better of it and wordlessly left the loft. When Valentina finally opened her eyes, the midwife stood over her, the baby in her arms. With great sadness she said, "Take your son now, Valentina. I need to go home and tend to my family, but I will be back to stay with you tonight." She too left the loft, and Valentina lay alone with the baby cradled in her arms. She listened to the stillness of the house, and felt her heart break. She suspected she would soon spend the rest of her days like this.

Chapter 18

Valentina closed her eyes and felt the sun hit her face. It was so good to be outside, away from her daily chores. She smiled down at the baby who lay flat on his belly in the grass, his attention completely focused on some ants carrying a crust of bread across the yard.

He was the only joy in her life now. After he'd been born, Antonio had withdrawn even more from her. He spent less time at home, dividing his days between the fields, caring for his mother, and the tavern where he would drown his sorrows in cheap wine. She frowned as she thought of Mrs. Fero. Valentina had felt enormous guilt at her stroke, thinking the news of the baby's paternity had caused her to become ill. But her mother-in-law was a hard, demanding woman. No amount of bad news would have been enough to debilitate her. Since her stroke she'd regained her speech, but remained bed-ridden, unable to see to her daily or personal needs without the help of one of her children.

Antonio held her responsible, of course, but she also suspected he blamed himself for her illness. He took turns with his brothers and sisters in seeing to her, and he made himself as available as he could whenever she needed something. Valentina had not dared to visit her since the stroke, in fear that she would be thrown out of her mother-in-law's house by one of her children, or worse, by Antonio himself.

John left home soon after the baby was born. He said goodbye to Valentina one afternoon as he and Miguel readied for their trip to Lisbon. "I intend to find a ship," John had explained when he told her of his plans to leave. "Miguel and I can work together and see the world without anyone persecuting our relationship. As long as we're discreet and careful, it might prove to be a much better adventure than the life we've had here." He frowned as he took in Valentina's disappointed expression. "I wish I could bring you with me," he said. Part of her wished she could go with them, but she knew her place was here, however uncertain it may be, and working on a ship was no life for a small child. With great sadness she'd watched another friend leave, and her heart broke all over again. First Ana, now John. Who else would abandon her here?

How she wished she had her guitar, but she did not want to get up and retrieve it while the baby was so intent on his examination. She hummed a song as she watched him poke at the anthill he'd discovered, his chubby fingers sneaking through the grass to upset the unsuspecting ants. He giggled as one tiny ant crawled across his thumb and disappeared inside the anthill. Her sweet boy was only six months old, but he was already so inquisitive. His silky blond hair shone almost white in the bright sun. He looked so much like Dimitri, she thought. Her heart ached as she remembered happier times. Dimitri would never know his son. It was a fact Valentina agonized over every day of her life.

"Time to go in." Valentina picked the baby up and brushed the grass from his clothes. His gummy smile tugged at her heart as she kissed the top of his head. "How proud your daddy would be of you," she whispered as she held him close. The baby's hand closed around the pendant at her neck. *He knows who his father is,* Valentina sighed. "If only I could tell you the truth," she said aloud. The baby tugged at the chain and laughed, the sweet sound like music in the small yard. She gently unclasped his hand from the necklace and tucked it back inside her dress. Someday she would give it to him as she told him of his real father. But for now, her love would have to be enough to keep Dimitri's memory alive for them both. She slowly turned and walked back to the house.

* * *

"I need to take the rent money to the landlord," Antonio announced after breakfast.

"When will you be back?" Valentina asked as she fed the baby.

"Tomorrow afternoon. I need to travel to the next village. Have supper ready for me." He rose from his seat and placed his cap on his head. "Good-bye Valentina."

"Wait." She stood and placed the baby in his cradle. "We need to talk," she said.

"I don't have time," he protested. "I need to leave now." He did not look at her as he spoke.

Frustrated, Valentina let out a weary sigh. "When would be a good time, Antonio? You're never home anymore. We can't keep going on like this. You can't ignore me or the baby forever."

"I'm doing the best I can," he muttered. "You can't ask more than that from me."

"I'm asking you to be my husband, and a father to our baby. You haven't been here to even try. You've always said that the marriage vows are sacred. Why can't you honor them now? Why must you turn away from your family?" Valentina wiped a stray tear from her cheek. She would not let another moment go by without telling him how she felt.

Antonio looked at her a long time, and then said, "I can't. I wanted to. God knows I wanted to try. But he's nothing like me…I can't be what I don't feel. And as for our marriage, I was wrong to take you from your village. I know that now and there's nothing I can do to change that. I provide for you and the baby. Don't ask any more of me."

"I only want you to love us," she replied quietly. "If that's too much to ask, say so and we'll go away."

"I do care for you, Valentina. I know we've never seen eye to eye, but I have always had feelings for you."

"And the baby?" She held her breath as she watched his expression, her hand on one hip in a restless gesture.

Finally, Antonio answered. "I've done all I can for the baby. I'm sorry it's not enough."

Valentina felt as though someone had stabbed a knife into her heart. "I love you, Antonio," she announced quietly. "Despite what we've been through, I have grown to love you."

A deep red stain flushed Antonio's cheeks, and he awkwardly leaned forward and brushed a soft kiss on Valentina's lips. "I need to go," he repeated. "We'll discuss this when I get back."

"Good-bye," she called out as he hastily left the house and mounted the donkey. She watched him ride out of the yard onto the road, her heart aching. She loved her husband even after all they'd been through. It had taken her a long time, but she now understood that there were different grades of love that one person could have for another. Her love for Dimitri was pure, sacred. Their innocence had been explored together, and their hearts had been filled with each other.

Antonio had deceived her to try and win her love. He took away everything she had, her family and friends, then grudgingly gave her enough to keep the peace between them. She had grown to appreciate his brooding manner and straightforward ways, though they still argued over a great deal. She had accepted that she could love her husband without being disloyal to her memories of Dimitri.

But the bitter irony was that Antonio did not love her. He could not even bring himself to say as much. And he certainly had no feelings for the baby. Defeated, she turned away and cleared the breakfast dishes. She felt so alone. Would it always be like this for her? she wondered.

* * *

When Antonio did not return the next night, Valentina wasn't concerned. He probably stopped at his mother's, or went for a drink in the village. She suspected he was not in the mood to face her and finish their conversation from the day before. But when he did not come home the next morning, she began to worry. Taking a deep breath, she told herself there was only one thing she could do. She wrapped the baby in a blanket and threw her shawl over her head. She then set out for her mother-in-law's house.

Her sister-in-law Sandra answered the door. "What do you want?" she sneered as Valentina looked around her into the house.

"Is Antonio here?" she asked. She was not going to let this woman upset her.

"No, he's not. Maybe he finally wised up and left you." She was about to slam the door in Valentina's face when a weak but clear voice commanded, "Let her in."

Silently Sandra stepped aside and Valentina entered the dark and cool house. The only light came from a lantern by the side of Mrs. Fero's bed, which had been moved to the center of the room. The older woman lay bundled in blankets, her bony hands resting at her sides. She motioned for Valentina to come closer, patting the edge of the bed. "Sit," she ordered, and Valentina obediently sat down.

Her speech impaired, she struggled with her words. "Where is my son?" she asked.

"I don't know. He hasn't returned from paying the rent yet," Valentina replied.

"Sandra," Antonio's mother called out. "Call your brother Manuel and tell him to go and look for Antonio. Perhaps he's at the tavern."

"Mrs. Fero," Valentina began.

The older woman shook her head. "I do this because he is my son, not because he is your husband." She raised a hand weakly and indicated the baby. "Let me see him."

Valentina pulled the blanket aside so she could see the baby, who was fast asleep. "He is a beautiful child," her mother-in-law decided. "It is a shame he does not carry Fero blood. My son has been good to you in caring for this child as his own."

Valentina thought it best not to argue with her. "Yes he has," she lied.

Sandra ran into the room and breathlessly announced, "There are some men outside with Manuel, and they have Antonio's donkey."

Valentina rose quickly, but a hand closed on her wrist. "Stay here," her mother-in-law commanded. To Sandra, she said, "Send them inside."

Valentina rose and said, "I sense Antonio is in danger. He may be your son, but he is also my husband."

Mrs. Fero's reply was interrupted by the arrival of the two men. They entered the room and immediately removed their hats. "*Bom dia*," they acknowledged.

Valentina felt a cold sense of dread wrap around her heart as she watched the men shift nervously before her. Antonio's mother did not miss their unease either. "Well, what do you know of my son?" she demanded.

"I'm sorry to tell you this," one of the men spoke, "but Antonio is dead."

Valentina felt the earth tilt violently. "What did you say?" she whispered.

The other man elaborated. "We met Antonio on the ridge overlooking the next village. He said he was headed home. It was dark, and we think he lost his footing."

"The donkey was spooked and raced down the ridge. Antonio had tied the reins to his wrist so he wouldn't lose the animal, and got dragged with it. We searched all night for him, and found him this morning. I'm really very sorry," the first man offered.

Antonio's mother went into shock and spoke no more.

Sandra ushered them out and she shut the door. "Poor Antonio," she cried. "He's gone, oh Mama, he's gone!"

Valentina thought her legs would give way. She wordlessly placed the baby on her mother-in-law's bed and attempted to get outside for air. But the door was too far away. It seemed Valentina would never reach it when the floor rushed up at her and the world went black.

* * *

Valentina was so distraught that she pretended to be asleep and listened as Antonio's brothers and sisters offered prayers and discussed preparations for the funeral. When she heard the priest's voice, she rose from the bed and sought out her infant son. She was surprised to see him in John's arms instead of with one of the many women who had gathered in the small room. John gently put the baby in Valentina's arms and guided them to a chair in the corner of the room. As the priest made his way to Valentina, a hush fell over the room.

"I know it's difficult," he began, "but you have youth on your side. Have courage, my child. God will give you the strength and wisdom to go on. Don't let anger take over your grief and destroy your soul."

Valentina only nodded numbly. As the day passed, she prayed alone for an hour to escape the chaos surrounding her. Once again someone she loved had left her. The burden of her loss pressed in on her until she thought she would suffocate. *Remember the baby,* she reminded herself constantly as the hours ticked by. He was all she had left.

* * *

Valentina adjusted the shawl on her head and studied the women around her. Her sisters-in-law carried trays piled high with food to and from the kitchen in preparation of the visitors they would receive after the funeral. The baby fussed in her arms, and Valentina carried him outside, anything to escape the oppressive atmosphere in the small house. She held him close as they passed a few of Antonio's friends, and they muttered their condolences as she walked by. She smiled her thanks, and then retreated for the safety of the backyard.

It had been a couple of days since Antonio's death. In that time she had had to endure several tongue-lashings from Antonio's sisters and father. It seemed everyone blamed her for his death. His sister Sandra had been especially cruel. "You think that because my brother is dead that I will support you now!" she'd said. Her angry eyes had bored into Valentina's, daring her to deny it.

"I want nothing from you," she'd answered, refusing to let this woman intimidate her.

"And that's exactly what you'll get—nothing. Not even for that little bastard you carry around."

Valentina had also been told in great detail how her mother-in-law had learned of the baby's true father. "You spoke to that salesman from *Arrifes*, didn't you?" her sister-in-law had accused. "She's not stupid, Valentina. She put it all together when he mentioned the doctor's son, Dimitri Maciel. How dare you pass off that child as one of my own flesh and blood! You'll pay for humiliating my family! You have a week to get out of here, and I never want to see you or your bastard again. As soon as the funeral is over, leave and don't come back."

She blinked back tears as she puzzled over where she might go. Home was out of the question. She had no family left there. Her mother and sister were now in America, and she didn't dare risk Dimitri's family finding out about the baby. One look at his little blond head and they would know for sure who his father is.

She could not stay here either. With no money or means of support, she would be at the mercy of a handout or charity from the church. She would not raise her son on the streets. There was only one other option, but she couldn't consider it just yet. There was still the funeral to get through.

"Valentina!" She looked up and tears spilled down her cheeks as Gabriela entered the yard, her husband Ernesto in tow. "I'm so sorry," she cried as she hugged her friend. Her husband did not seem to notice their acquaintance. He was too busy helping himself to a cigarette from his jacket pocket.

"Thank you for being here," Valentina sniffed. At least there was one person here who did not hate her.

"Ernesto worked with Antonio in the fields. He had to come, to give his condolences, and dragged me along. Of course I pretended to come along reluctantly," she managed to grin. She reached for the baby and asked to hold him. A look of intense longing crossed her face. "I'd always hoped to have a baby of my own one day," she sighed as she nuzzled the baby's cheek. "Fate decided otherwise." She glanced at Ernesto as she said this. Somehow in the course of a few minutes, he'd managed to find a very large glass of wine, and was speaking to some of his friends near the back door of the house.

"My baby is the world to me," Valentina declared as Gabriela handed him back. "I have nothing else."

"What will you do now?" Gabriela was well aware of the family's edict that Valentina had to leave by the end of the funeral.

"I don't know. I was thinking of going to America," she replied quietly.

"America! How? Where will you get the money?" Gabriela asked. A movement behind Valentina caught her eye, and Gabriela suddenly smiled. "I know how," she said.

Valentina turned and saw Augusto Ponte enter the yard. He nodded at his brother and the other men, and then walked towards the two women. "I'm very sorry, Valentina," he said.

"Thank you." What had Gabriela meant when she said she knew how Valentina would get to America? "I appreciate your coming today," she added.

"I thought you might need the support. These vultures are only out for themselves." He studied Valentina a moment, coming to some sort of decision. "Come see me tomorrow. I think I may be able to help you," he said mysteriously. He tipped his hat at them and walked away.

"What was that all about?" Valentina wondered aloud.

But Gabriela was already making plans. She knew what she would have to do to help her friend.

* * *

The priest shook her hand and offered his sympathies, but all Valentina could see in front of her was the covered body of her husband on a bed in the center of the room. The white sheet did little to hide the broken and decaying state he was in. Flies swarmed around it, and the warm air was pungent with the suffocating smell of death. She wanted to run for the door, away from this nightmare, but knew she had to withstand another hour of friendly courtesy as one by one, every friend, enemy, and relative Antonio ever had marched through the room.

The food tables creaked under the weight of so much to eat, and here too the flies had taken up residence. She watched in horror as one of her nephews popped a pastry in his mouth, bugs and all. "This is sick," she mumbled.

"Excuse me?" asked the priest. "Did you say you are sick?"

"No." She pushed past him and ran outside, drawing in huge gulps of air. She sank down into the grass and pulled her knees up to her chest. The baby slept safely in her mother-in-law's old bedroom, so she took these few moments to simply think.

Antonio was dead. She had finally come to love her husband, a choice she had made willingly. They had never been as close as a husband and wife should be, and she remembered what she'd said to him one day after a particularly bad argument. She had said that his insecurities would be the death of him, and she had been right. He had died still confused over his feelings for her, and still in denial about the life they could have led. Now there was no going back. She could not undo the past few months, but she would not subject herself, or her son, to the misery and poverty that waited if she remained here. Her bags were already packed, and John had immediately offered her a place to stay tonight at Miguel's family's house. He had come immediately when he heard about Antonio, the only one of the Feros who did not blame her in some way for his brother's death.

The day after the funeral Valentina wanted to say her last good-byes in privacy. It was quiet and peaceful as she climbed the incline to the village cemetery, stopping frequently and picking up wildflowers on the way. Once she went through the gated entrance, she stopped and scanned the graves for the fresh mound of dirt. *There it was.* Silently she approached and laid the hand-molded bouquet of wildflowers at the foot of Antonio's grave. After a few minutes of reverent prayers of regrets and sorrow, Valentina left the same way she came in, somber and unsure of her future. But there was one thing she knew she had to do. She would go to America. There was no other way.

Chapter 19

"Are you sure about this?" Valentina sidestepped an exposed tree root and nearly landed on her backside. "He lives out here?" she asked as she waved an arm to encircle their surroundings. They stood in the middle of the forest behind Valentina's old house. It was the farthest away she'd ever been from home since she'd arrived there. "Does he live in a cave?" she grumbled as she swiped at a low tree branch.

"Augusto is also a forest ranger. I explained all of this to you, remember?" Gabriela stole a look around them. If her husband knew she was here, he'd beat her senseless. She shivered at the thought, but pasted a smile on her face for her worried friend. "We're not lost, so don't worry. I know the way." It was not the first time she had guided someone in need to Augusto's door, and she knew it wouldn't be the last. "This way." She pointed to a narrow trail overrun with bushes. "We need to get there before he leaves for the day."

They continued on their way, careful not to wander too far from each other. Eventually the path led up to a long wooden building nestled within a thick stand of trees. Gabriela approached the door and knocked loudly. They could hear footsteps on the other side, and the door creaked open.

"*Bom dia* ladies. I see you took me up on my offer." Augusto motioned them inside and shut the door. He pulled a bench from the wall into the center of the room and asked them to sit down. "Where is the baby?" he inquired.

"He's with my brother-in-law John," Valentina replied. She had not thought it would be a good idea to bring him on the trip. "I need your help," she said quietly. But would he be able to help her?

Augusto paced the room, his expression unreadable. Finally, he stopped before them and said, "You must go to America. There is no other way, Valentina. Antonio's family will not protect you now."

"I know." She had debated again the night before as she lay huddled with the baby on Miguel's family's floor, a blanket the only barrier between her and the cold dirt. She wished there were an easier way to spare her son the hardship ahead, but she also knew that if they remained in *Furnas*, he would be ridiculed, and eventually suffer the shame of not being Antonio's son. She could not do that to him. America was her only choice now.

"I can help you, Valentina. You will not have to go through this alone." He outlined his plan to them. He would acquire the money she needed for her and the baby to sail out of *Ponta Delgada,* and a little extra to get her settled once she reached New York. He would also get their papers in order. "What is the boy's name?" he asked.

Valentina took a deep breath. She had always called her son by name, but everyone else knew him as "the baby." She had not wanted to reveal it until the time was right. "His name is Joshua," she replied, "Joshua Dimitri Marques."

Augusto raised an eyebrow but said nothing. "Tomorrow we will go and register your son, and I will have the papers drawn up for you and the baby…Joshua," he smiled. "I will bring everything to you tomorrow. Now go home to your son and say your good-byes, Valentina. By Friday you will be sailing to America."

Valentina stood and shook his hand. "Thank you so much," she said, holding back tears.

"Anything to help," he replied solemnly. "I know how difficult life has been here for you. It is time that you had a better way of it. Take care." He looked at Gabriela and said, "The same goes for you as well."

Gabriela blushed, and Valentina did not miss the gentle way Augusto addressed his sister-in-law, but she remained quiet. "Good-bye, Augusto."

"Good-bye ladies." He opened the door for them and held it as they exited, then closed it quietly behind them.

"What was that all about?" Valentina demanded as they walked back through the forest.

"What was what?" Gabriela asked coyly.

"You know very well what I mean," Valentina countered. "I saw the way Augusto looked at you."

"He's very good to me," Gabriela answered vaguely. She quickly changed the subject. "Are you excited yet?" she asked her friend.

"A little. But mostly I'm just scared." What would she do in America? Would she be able to work? And what about a home for her and the baby? Her mother could not be counted on for help. She had her own struggles to deal with. Valentina was on her own. "I don't know if I'm ready for this," she confided. "I just lost Antonio. How will I manage without him here?"

"The same you managed all this time, Valentina. He was never really there for you. Why would now be different? Antonio and Ernesto were cut from the same cloth. They thought only of themselves. No one else mattered. He never cared about you the way you'd hoped he would."

"I know that, but I still feel guilty. He's only been gone a week, and now I'm leaving everything behind." Valentina stepped over a large rock in her path. "I feel like I'm abandoning him.

"He abandoned you and the baby a long time ago. And you're leaving behind exactly what he left you—nothing." Gabriela reached the ridge and hugged her friend. "I'll see you tomorrow. Good luck Valentina."

"Thank you, Gabriela. You've been a true friend." Tears streamed down her face as she added, "I will miss you so much."

"Me too. Now go home before I start crying all over the place!" Gabriela waved and turned back to the forest.

"Good-bye, my friend," Valentina whispered as she waved back. Once again she would lose someone she cared for. But would life in America bring her the joy she desperately sought?

* * *

Valentina stood by the door, nervous. She held Joshua tightly in her arms, her shawl covering them both. Today she would register her son and finalize her plans for America. Excitement and sadness warred within her as she watched Augusto stroll down the street toward Miguel's family's home. This was the only way, she realized. She knew she had to secure a future for herself and her son. But she was also leaving behind her friends, the only people who had ever made her feel welcome in this small, poor village.

"Are you ready?" Augusto asked as he reached the door. He took in her shrouded appearance. "There are no clothing restrictions in the law manuals that I know of, Valentina," he joked. "You can uncover yourself and Joshua."

"I don't know if that's such a good idea." Valentina had avoided going into the village square after Joshua was born. The Feros had done a thorough job of making sure everyone knew Antonio wasn't the baby's father. She did not want to face the curiosity and ridicule she was sure would follow her as she tried to live a normal, everyday life in *Furnas*. She knew that by removing the shawl, she would be lifting the veil that protectively shielded her son from the gawkers of the village.

"Trust me, you have nothing to fear. You can remove it." Augusto held the baby as she pulled the shawl free and left it in the house. She reached for Joshua and the three of them headed out.

"I must tell you Valentina, that there is a small problem with Joshua's name." Augusto crossed the street and nodded to some of the villagers.

The man stared open-mouthed, one hand on his hoe, while his wife elbowed him in the ribs and whispered, "You see that, Manuel? That's Antonio Fero's widow and her illegitimate son."

"What's wrong with his name?" Valentina asked. She held her head high, undaunted by the rude villagers.

"Because he'll be named Marques, and not Fero, the priest won't baptize him," Augusto explained.

"It doesn't matter," she replied. "I don't need his approval, or anyone else's. God approved of my love for Joshua's father the day my son was conceived, and that's all I need."

"You're right Valentina, that is all you need," he smiled.

They rounded a corner and Valentina came face to face with her sister-in-law Sandra.

"Oh Mother of God!" Sandra exclaimed as she fell back against the stone wall and placed a hand over her heart. "If it isn't the village tramp! And look who she's got with her, the self-appointed magistrate! What's the matter, Augusto? Didn't you have any stray dogs to save today? Oh wait, you found this one," she taunted as she stared at Valentina.

"Watch yourself, Sandra Melo. Your husband wouldn't appreciate you running your mouth off in the village," Augusto warned.

Sandra visibly paled at the mention of her husband, another local whose reputation rivaled that of his brother Ernesto's. "You think you can draw strength from him, Valentina? Do you think Augusto can protect you? You are totally without shame if you think you can strut around the village like a proud peacock and no one will talk."

"I think that's enough Sandra. Go home." Augusto's voice was firm, and Sandra involuntarily backed away from them.

"You think you're bold and courageous, Valentina, and you carry that golden-haired bastard of yours high on your chest like a trophy. No wonder my brother is dead. He did it to escape you, you *puta*!"

Augusto was furious. "Enough!" A small crowd had gathered around them, their attention fixed on the drama playing out before them. "You have said your peace. Now let us pass." He didn't wait for a reply. Augusto took Valentina by the elbow and they continued down the street.

"Thank you for standing up for me," Valentina said.

"I could do no less. She had no right to speak to you that way."

Valentina nodded her head, but her heart told her otherwise. She had shamed Antonio's family, even though Antonio had married her with the knowledge that she was already pregnant. His family couldn't help but be angry.

"Valentina." They had stopped in front of the Civil Registry, and Augusto faced her. "She had no right. You were very brave not to retaliate over the hurtful things she said," he reminded her.

"I had to protect Joshua." This was all for him, and no one would cheat him out of the life he deserved.

He regarded her a moment, then smiled. "Let's go register your boy," he said as he held open the door and Valentina stepped inside.

The process went relatively quickly, and when they emerged

from the registry an hour later, Valentina and Joshua were cleared to set sail for America. "I can't believe it," she admitted as they headed back to Miguel's house.

"You deserve this, Valentina. It's your time to have a good life for you and your son," Augusto replied.

On the way back, Valentina noted with amazement that the villagers were considerably kinder to her. The men tipped their hats and the women smiled in greeting. Some even ventured a tentative, "*Bom dia.*" She knew this was because of Augusto, but it gave her a certain satisfaction that she could earn their respect before she left for America.

"Until Friday, Valentina," Augusto said as he left her at her door.

"Friday," she nodded. "And thank you," she called out. Soon they would be on their way to a new life. Valentina brushed a kiss over Joshua's blond head and thanked God for answering her prayers.

* * *

"I will miss you, Valentina," John said as he hugged his sister-in-law. He kissed the baby's forehead and held him close for a moment. "Good luck to you in America."

"Thank you John." She smiled at his companion, Miguel, who waited quietly behind him.

The other man cleared his throat and said, "Good luck to you both."

"I hope I'm making the right decision." She glanced over at the cart that held her few belongings. Augusto had arrived early that morning with papers and money in hand, and had said he would personally take her to the capital city to see her off. Gabriela had instantly agreed to go with them.

"But what about Ernesto?" Valentina asked, alarmed.

"What about him?" Valentina watched in shock as Augusto took Gabriela's hand in his and kissed it. "I've decided it's time I start living my own life," she explained as she smiled at him. "You taught me that, Valentina, and I can never thank you enough for it."

Now she stood with the only other person who had ever made her feel welcome in this small village, and gave him one last hug. "Be happy," she sniffed. "Never let anyone deny you the right to be as unique as you are."

"I won't." John slipped some money into her hand and said, "For the baby. Think of it as a godfather's present," he said when she protested.

She wiped at the tears that spilled down her cheeks. "You've been so good to me."

"And you've been good to me as well, Valentina. Never forget to remain as unique as you are either." He helped her into the cart and waved farewell. "Good luck," he called out.

I'm going to need it, she thought as they rolled away from the yard. She held little Joshua close. "We're off to America," she whispered into his ear.

Joshua looked up at her and smiled.

Chapter 20

Valentina stared up at the large ship, sadness in her heart. When she left *Arrifes* she had also left the man who had been the love of her life. She had always had a glimmer of hope that some day their paths would cross, that she would see Dimitri's face one more time. Now all her hopes were lost.

She boarded the ship, holding tightly to Joshua, who hid his face in his mother's shawl. It took Valentina a while to absorb the grandeur of her surroundings. Her emotions warred with her, from excitement at going to a new country, to a mixture of confusion and uncertainty, not knowing if life would be any better in a foreign place. She waved one last time to Augusto and Gabriela. Somewhere in all this those two found each other, and she did not doubt that Augusto would move heaven and earth for the woman he loved. It broke her heart to think that Dimitri would have done the same if she had been honest with him. She stood and watched her friends until the ship was too far out and they were only tiny pinpoints on the distant shore.

On the first day some gulls had squawked by the ship, but now as Valentina leaned over the rail, the only sound she heard was the gentle splashing of the waves against the ship's hull. For days, all she would see was water and sky. Some days on board were unbearably hot, and Valentina wore a single layer of loose white cotton, a dress that she had once worn long before she ever became Mrs. Antonio Fero. Her breasts were no longer bound, making them hang slightly, but she noticed they were not as full as they had been when they were filled with the precious life milk needed to sustain her son. So much had changed in so short a time. She reached for the pendant that she still wore around her neck, and thought of Dimitri. In a trance she would touch it to her lips in remembrance of the kisses they shared and would wish for what she knew could never happen.

To soothe herself and Joshua, she would bring her guitar on deck and sing, drawing the people who were on deck enjoying the breeze of the evening. They would sit around her, and she made some new friends, finding that they too were anxious about their new country. When it grew too dark to be outside, she picked up the baby and her guitar and headed for her bed, pausing before opening the glass door. She studied her reflection, the reflection of a woman, and not the carefree girl of so long ago.

The trip was long and tiring, and when Valentina was not walking the deck or entertaining the other passengers, she was writing. To make the adjustment easier, she wrote to her mother and explained in detail Joshua's birth and the circumstances surrounding it. She did not think her mother would be able to help her much once she arrived in America, but she had to be honest with her. Life in this new country would hopefully be better than the one she left behind, but she did not expect that to happen overnight.

* * *

The ship finally docked at Ellis Island some weeks later. Debarkation was a tedious, slow process. Valentina arrived with her son, but unlike the other passengers who strolled through the crowd looking for familiar faces of family waiting for them,

Valentina would find none. A new beginning in a new country, she thought to herself. She debated whether she had made the right decision, but it really was an opportunity for a new start. She looked down at Joshua, but he was so tired that she decided to sit and wait for the crowd to thin out a little. Eventually she saw her chance and approached one of the lines that led to registration. As she arrived at the guard's table, she felt a moment of fear. Here she was, again an alien in a new place. "Name?" the guard asked as she set down her bag and adjusted the baby on her hip.

"Valentina Marques," she replied. "And this is my son, Joshua Dimitri Marques." She had practiced her English while on board the ship, with the help of an American woman traveling home after visiting relatives in *Mosteiros*. It was still rather broken, but by simply saying her name in the language of her new home, Valentina felt a glimmer of hope she had not known until that moment.

The guard made a notation in the ledger in front of him. "Check your papers there," he said in reasonable Portuguese. Valentina thanked him and moved on to the next checkpoint. She watched as they roughly handled her bags and checked her and the baby for contraband. By the time she emerged from the dark and crowded building, it was well past lunchtime, and she and the baby were starved.

"Valentina Marques?" called an unfamiliar voice. She turned and saw an elderly man shuffle towards her. "Augusto said you'd be arriving today," he explained as he shook her hand. "My name is Eduardo Vasconcellos. Please come with me."

She followed him to a horse-drawn cart and he placed her things in the back. He held the baby as she climbed up, then placed little Joshua in her arms. "Time to take you home," he said as he flicked the reins and rumbled off.

Valentina looked around her, astonished. America was a grand place indeed. There were so many lights; long, wide roads, tall buildings, and the houses weren't side by side like in the village, but one on top of the other. Eduardo called them apartments. It was also very cold. Valentina had never seen snow, and was awestruck by the piles of white powder lying across the landscape, so white that it blurred her vision. Joshua lay tucked against her, his soft blond hair peeking out through the folds of the blanket. He opened his eyes briefly, and she was struck by their color, as intense as the sea blue eyes of his father.

Eduardo stopped the cart in front of a tall, red brick building. "We're here!" he announced as he climbed down and helped her out of the cart. He reached for her things while she climbed the front steps. He opened the door and she followed him up another flight of stairs to her mother's apartment on the second floor.

"Valentina, you're here!" her mother cried as the door flew open. Mother and daughter squeezed each other in a tight hug, Joshua forgotten until he wailed in between them.

Valentina stepped back and unwrapped his blanket. "This is your grandson Joshua," she said. Pale, soft, yellow curls surrounded his pudgy face, and his big blue eyes took in this stranger that his mother was hugging.

"Come to *Vavó*," his grandmother said as she lifted him into her arms and hugged him tight. Caressing and touching the boy's hair, she looked up and said, "It's soft as silk." She then closed her eyes and whispered, "He looks just like Dimitri. I'm glad you wrote me and prepared me for this, Valentina. I had thought Antonio was Joshua's father. You broke Ana's heart when you married him, you know."

Valentina could not bring herself to speak. She entered her mother's home and immediately spied what her mother said was a sofa. She sat down and bounced on it like a child. "Mama, are you rich?" she asked as she felt the soft fabric of it around her. These were not the hard benches of her home in *Furnas*. She leaned back and enjoyed the comfort of such a luxurious possession.

"No," her mother replied. Valentina noticed that her mother looked much older than when she'd last seen her. "I live week to week and do the best I can. Although I live comfortably here, I still miss home. But with you here it will be easier."

"Where is my sister?" Valentina rose and took Joshua in her arms. It was time to feed him. Her mother led the way to the kitchen. A box stood in one corner, and her mother called it an icebox. From inside she withdrew a bottle of milk and placed it on the table. "Your sister got married to a very nice boy from Queens, not too far from here. She comes to visit when she can." She poured the milk into a mug and Valentina held it to the baby's lips. He drank greedily, and she marveled at how modern everything here was compared to home.

"Who is the man who brought me here?" Valentina asked as she set the mug aside and wiped the baby's chin.

"Eduardo lives downstairs with his wife Cecelia. He's very good friends with the man you wrote me about, Augusto Ponte." Her mother placed the milk back inside the icebox and reached for an iron kettle on top of a contraption she called a stove. She filled it from a faucet over a deep sink and replaced it on the stove's surface. She lit the fire beneath and said brightly, "I'll make us some tea."

They spent the afternoon talking and catching up. Valentina's mother apologized for her treatment of her daughter the day she left home. "I wanted you to be ready for your new life. I knew it would not be easy for you. I did not want to send you off with any illusions about the kind of life you would be living."

"I understand now. I just wish that I had chosen differently," Valentina replied sadly.

"You know you could not have had a life with Dimitri Maciel.

His family was too rich, too powerful. They would never have accepted you, and they would have made life very difficult for Joshua, maybe even taken him away from you. You have a new life here now. You might meet a nice man and settle down again," her mother suggested. "You are still young. Perhaps love waits for you yet."

"Perhaps." But if his name wasn't Dimitri Maciel, she didn't want to have anything to do with men for the rest of her life. "Joshua and I will be fine," she added, more to reassure herself than anyone else.

* * *

Valentina went to work a week later in a cotton mill with her mother. She worked very hard during the day, and at night she took in seamstress work from the women in the neighborhood. Eventually word of her skill spread, and every dime she could manage to save she put away for the future. After only two years, she had saved enough money to start her own business, something unheard of for a woman in the small community she now called home. With her mother's help and encouragement from her many clients, Valentina opened her shop, Valentina's Bridal Boutique. Bridal gowns were her specialty, and with her mother's embroidery expertise Valentina designed a pattern for a signature gown. The realization of the wedding gown of her dreams was bittersweet. It became her most requested bestseller, but it was a gown she would never wear.

* * *

Her child, her son. He was Valentina's everything. Sweet, innocent, he was the flesh of her flesh. He curled his little finger around her long index finger, and together they strolled down one of the more fashionable neighborhoods in the city. She felt so carefree, with the cool breeze blowing Joshua's curls back away from his face. He will be tall like his father, she thought as she watched him point to a passing butterfly and laugh. His eyes were replicas of Dimitri's own, their color as vibrant as the blue sky. He had inherited his father's genes: tall, blond, blue-eyed, but she feared he would inherit some of his paternal grandparents' less admirable traits and grow up with too much sense of pride. She would instill humility in him, Valentina determined. She would never want him to think himself too good for any woman.

It was while they walked and she contemplated her thoughts that Valentina found the perfect house. Built in the 1800s, it was an old house, but it had character. It needed a little loving care, she realized as she examined the crumbling paint and broken shutters. But she wanted the big Victorian house with three floors. The first floor would be for her stock and show room. The third floor maid's quarters would be her mother's living quarters, and Valentina would take the second floor as her living space. A veranda ran the length of the house, the perfect place to sit and drink a quiet cup of tea on a warm spring day. The pointed roof reminded her of a witch's peaked hat, and thick, round columns stood like sentinels, supporting both the roof and the upper floors. "It's absolutely perfect," she breathed.

Joshua looked up at her and smiled, his gap tooth grin filling her heart with joy. Despite the odds, she had come to a new country, made a success of herself, and now she would provide a real home for her family, all without relying on a man to help her. "Let's go tell *Vavó*," she said as she swept Joshua into her arms and headed back to the apartment.

* * *

A few weeks later Valentina unlocked the front door of her new home. Once inside, she began to make plans. "The grand foyer will make a perfect display entrance," she explained as the carpenter behind her dutifully took notes. It led to a round staircase with a landing in the middle, and a floor to ceiling stained glass window. The connecting room had an enormous fireplace, which would make an inviting display room. It was part of a double parlor that connected with pocket doors. "I'll use this room for the privacy of the bridal fittings," she said. The carpenter scribbled into his pad as she called out paint colors, wallpaper and carpet ideas as they walked through each room.

She would spend her entire savings on the house. She visited an antique shop and there she noticed in a dark corner, draped with cobwebs, the most unusual brass candleholders that stood four feet high. She knew she had to buy them. They would look perfect by the fireplace. Other beautiful things slowly found a new home in the grand Victorian. When the repairs were done a reporter from the local newspaper came to do a story on the house. It had made the front page, and the heading stated "it was one of the finest restorations in the area."

But it was the outside of the house that appealed to her the most. An old, weathered carriage house sat on the grounds, covered with grape vines, and overgrown with old shrubs and lots of shade trees. It would make the perfect playhouse for her son. Her heart hammered in her chest as Valentina realized that she had been meant to buy this house. Life would become easier for Joshua, her mother, and herself. Valentina had accepted herself and her limited means. She was grateful and felt privileged to have learned the skill needed to do the kind of work that she was doing. She would devote all her time and energy to her creations and making her life work for her family. Life was that in which we chose to live it. Business was good, and she did not have to struggle week to week anymore. She had been gifted with the art of music, and she had always thought she would make her fortune with it. It had been her childhood expectation. But her drive to be self-supportive and the desire for material success overruled any childish fantasies. She had rid herself of that unrealistic dream, and had found a new calling instead.

But her heart always remained unsettled. It was a blessing to be able to provide so much when she had started out with so little, but how wonderful would it have been if she could have shared it all with Dimitri. As she readied for bed each night, Valentina said a small prayer that wherever he was, he might be happy. She tried not to think that his happiness might include a wife and children to love. He had given her a beautiful son, and that would have to be enough.

Valentina was in her thirties, too young to be so lonely, and yet she knew it was her fault. She never put herself in a position to meet available men. And the ones she did meet did not interest her. Since she was a young girl she'd been told how beautiful she was, and after Joshua's birth, her stomach had returned to its flat state and her body had remained firm. She wore no make up and she had a natural glow in her face. She had a confident, passionate attitude that worked against her because it intimidated the men she did meet. She was a businesswoman in a man's world. Her days were busy but her nights were lonely, filled with her soft humming and the playing of her guitar. She had been in love once, a perfect love that she had shared with Dimitri in every way. Even her mother had given up on the idea of her ever finding a husband. "You're looking for the kind of love that you're touched by only once," she'd scolded Valentina. Perhaps she was right. After coming to America, Valentina had resigned herself to being alone.

Chapter 21

Valentina made a good life for her family, and even managed to put money away to send Joshua to college. Early on he had demonstrated an interest in medicine, and she knew she would do whatever it took to afford him the opportunity to follow in his father's footsteps. Valentina knew in her heart of hearts that eventually Joshua would be old enough and he'd leave home to pursue his studies. She also knew that she would have to tell him of Dimitri very soon. It was a decision she had debated for some time, but she would no longer keep any secrets from her son. He had a right to know. He was an intelligent boy, and would often ask her why he looked different from her and his grandmother. She had put him off for a long time with vague excuses, but she couldn't anymore. She fingered the pendant at her neck. "It's time," she whispered. Joshua needed to know who his father was. She had done her best to shape him into the man he had become, but there were parts of him that mirrored Dimitri so well that she could deny her son his heritage any longer. He may not want to hear what she had to say, but Valentina had no choice. While she still had courage to speak, she would tell him.

* * *

"Joshua, we need to talk."

"What is it Mother?" Joshua looked up from the book he was reading. At eighteen, he was the spitting image of his father. "What's troubling you?" he asked gently.

Valentina sat in the chair opposite him at the dining room table and folded her hands on top of it. She idly remembered sitting at a similar table many years before, when Joshua's grandmother had told her to forget Dimitri and marry Antonio. "It's about your father," she began. "Up until now you were too young to understand my sorrow, but in this adult world I can no longer shield you. You'll be leaving for school soon, and I need you to know the truth. I diluted it for years because I worried that I couldn't handle your disapproval. I made the journey to America to escape the hostility that society would have shown us."

"What are you saying?" Joshua stared into her eyes, suddenly unsure he wanted to know what his mother meant. "I'm not sure I want to hear this," he muttered.

"Joshua, please listen to reason." *This was so hard*, she thought miserably, but she pushed on. "I felt guilty for years over what I did to you, but that guilt diminished as you grew up with a strong and unique personality. I brought a child into this cruel world. You were the product of two people in love. But what could I have done? I lived in a tunnel of darkness, filled with depressive thoughts. I wanted to spare that pain from you." Feeling defeated, she closed her eyes and let her tears fall silently, her hand around Dimitri's pendant. "I never wanted to hurt you with the truth, Joshua. Antonio was not your father."

Joshua looked as though he'd been slapped. "What did you say?"

"Antonio Fero was not your father. I married him when I realized that your real father's parents would never accept me or you because we were poor. Please don't be angry," she pleaded.

"He never knew about you. I was afraid to say anything, and married Antonio instead."

Joshua flung out his hand, furious. "I don't want to know who he is. It's irrelevant now," he snapped. "Anyone can father a baby. It takes a real man to actually be a father." His tone softened as he took in his mother's distress. "I'm not mad at you, Mother," he said softly. "I just need time to absorb all this."

"I know." Valentina wiped her eyes and smiled at her son. "I obeyed the law of reason instead of obeying my heart."

"Mother," Joshua said as he came around to the other side of the table and drew her into a hug, "you put a roof over my head and food on the table every day. What I see is a woman of amazing courage and self-sacrificing devotion to her son. Over the years you've built a fortress around us, a bond where no one, nor anything you have to say to me can penetrate it."

"I love you so much, Joshua. And I know that it's always been you and me struggling along in this world. But I do need to tell you about your father."

"Please don't," he said, his anger and grief at war within him. He ran a hand through his hair and studied his mother's pained expression.

"So this is why you never remarried?" he questioned. "You never got over this man?" When she nodded, he went on. "My analysis is that he was a weakling to let you marry Antonio. He chose to give you up rather than face any quarrels with his mother and father. He was a coward, Mother. You've given me a look into this man's soul, and all I see is a man concerned with other people's opinions. But," he concluded, his expression thoughtful, "at least now I can understand the origin of the turmoil in your life."

"You sound like a psychiatrist," she laughed.

"I'm just being honest," he replied. "Your feelings of

inferiority came from this process of self-underestimation, making you feel unworthy. My father stood by and watched everyone destroy your will."

"Please, Joshua, you're filling your heart with hate for man you don't know or even understand." She took his hands in hers and tried to appeal to reason. "Here you've been exposed to a different culture. I chose the struggle and the sacrificial living to give you this better life. I chose to take a leap of faith and to trust it. I grew in wisdom, and it's that wisdom and guidance that I've passed on to you. Don't blame him for my decisions."

She released his hands and removed the pendant around her neck. She placed it in his hand and closed his fingers around it. "I never told him about you," she repeated. "I followed my deepest instincts. I knew in my heart and mind that my destiny was carved out for me."

His facial muscles tense, he grunted out, "Mother, you don't know how angry this makes me feel. He could have taken control of the situation. You were eighteen years old and you carried the weight of the world on your shoulders. You didn't trust him to make the right decision and that's why you did what you did. You loved him so much that you sacrificed a separation from your family marked by an enormous distance. Your detachment should have fueled his energy to fight for you. How can I forgive that?" he demanded.

"So I was conceived in an orchard," he went on, his eyes taking on a far away look. He remembered the necklace his mother had placed in his hand and looked down at it. The tiny soccer ball glistened in the sunlight streaming through the dining room windows. "This was his?" he asked.

"He gave it to me to remember him by. And now I'd like you to have it. It's all I have of your father," Valentina replied.

He slipped it over his head and tucked it inside his shirt. "For you Mother," he said. "I'll wear it for you. But my father probably knew you better than *Vavó* even did. And yet, while I developed legs, arms, and a heart within your womb, he didn't recognize any changes in you. Your heart knows your own passions," he sighed. "When you love someone, you're bound to each other. It's as simple as that."

"I wish it were son," Valentina answered, her heart lighter than it had been in years. She had told her son the truth. He did not yet understand the full weight of what she'd said, but time would tell. She hugged him to her and kissed his forehead. "You're so much like him. He went on to study medicine, just like you will. I think that he would be very proud of you."

"I guess I'll never know," Joshua replied sarcastically. He immediately regretted his tone when he saw his mother's expression crumble. "I'm sorry Mother. I'll try to understand."

"Thank you, Joshua. I know you will," she said.

Chapter 22

Joshua was leaving for school today.

Valentina knew that saying good-bye to her son was not going to easy, but he was a man now, paving the road to his own destiny. "All you see right now is study and hard work," she said. "With your education, you will be escaping the harsh realities of a poor man's way of life. There will be happiness in your future. You are young and kind. Don't be swayed by foolish ideas."

With tear-filled eyes, Joshua replied, "I will be gone from you Mother, but I will always hold you close in my heart."

When they embraced, Joshua lifted Valentina off the floor. With her arms wrapped tightly around him and her face buried in the crook of his neck, she said meekly, "I ask only one thing of you. Please find it in your heart to forgive the father you never met. It was by my choice, not his. It's not healthy for you to hold a grudge."

Eyes filled with tears, Joshua replied, "I love you and I'm proud to have you as my mother. I'll try to do this for you."

* * *

Joshua breezed through his four years of college, and in medical school he excelled in every subject. But he still couldn't shake off the resentment in his heart for his father. It did not matter that he had never met the man who sired him. It was enough to know that he had not cared to defend the woman he claimed to love. This fact burned in Joshua's heart each day as he studied and grew into a man he hoped his mother could be proud of, and one he prayed wouldn't remind her too much of the man she left behind.

He decided to do his internship at St. Andrew's Hospital, which was not far from home. He wanted to put the business with his father behind him, and hoped that everything would be the way it had always been with his mother. As he watched the landscape fly by from his window seat on the train that carried him home, Joshua allowed himself to once more reflect on the mystery man whose blood flowed in his veins. What kind of man was he to have his way with his mother? Joshua shook his head as he pictured her, back aching and hands raw as she would come in from the mill in those early days. His father had drunk from the same cup of ecstasy as she had, but the fate of young love was cut short. "When she announces that she's going to marry another man, he backs off," he muttered. For him, his father had two choices, courage or cowardice. For his mother it had been an unbearable and painful separation. Slowly he had watched her lift away the cobwebs of self-pity over the years, until the strong and successful woman he knew today had finally shone through.

But now I'm consumed with feelings of guilt for putting her in a position where she had to defend him, he thought angrily. He felt helpless over his confusing thoughts. He recognized the truth deep within, and knew that it would not be easy to see past. "I hate him so much," he whispered against the glass. Outside, the fresh green promise of spring streaked by, a reminder that all things must die to be reborn again. He feared that his mother had once loved this man, and that love was still alive in her heart, unable to be laid to rest so she could find love with someone else.

"I'll never express my feelings to her," he decided as he felt the train begin to slow down. Soon he would be home, and he would have to face her questions, but he couldn't share his doubts with her. "It's going to be a slow healing process." There was just no way around it.

* * *

His return home had been joyous. His mother could not stop hugging him or asking about school. She had wisely chosen to remain silent on the issue of his father, and Joshua had not volunteered any information either. Quickly they fell back into their old routines. After only a few days home, however, Joshua had to begin his internship. He would be working under a prestigious doctor at the hospital, but knew nothing else about him. He elected to meet the man at his home after the doctor had extended an invitation to him. He found himself standing on the porch of a large, stately house only two blocks from his own, his palms sweaty and his knees shaking slightly. This was what he had worked toward for six long years. He rang the bell and the door was opened by a petite, kind-faced woman who introduced herself as Marta. She looked at him oddly for a moment, as if she'd seen a ghost, but smiled and asked him to follow her inside.

She entered what appeared to be a study and announced, "Doctor, your new intern is here."

* * *

Dimitri turned away from the bookshelf he was examining and smiled at the young man. He did a double take at the tall, good-looking blonde man before him with a trim, athletic build. "Please come in," he managed, shaken at the young man's resemblance to himself. "My name is Dr. Maciel." He shook the intern's hand and felt the strength in it. He sat down in the black leather swivel chair behind the desk and motioned for his guest to take a seat as well. "You look very familiar," Dimitri said slowly. "Have you worked in the hospital as a technician?"

"No, this is my first internship," Joshua replied. He noted that his new employer bore a strange familiarity to him, but said nothing. It was an odd coincidence though, but Joshua had more important things to worry about, like making a good impression. He brushed off his thoughts and focused on his visit.

Dimitri stared in silence at Joshua Marques, his new intern. He'd invited him over so they could talk about his new position, but Dimitri found he was at a loss for words. Not only did Joshua look strikingly familiar, but his expressions mimicked his own. As he studied Joshua more closely, he noticed the widow's peak of almost white hair in the center of his forehead, the thick curving brows so much like his own, and the square, strong chin. Joshua Marques...Valentina...

Recognition hit like lightning as he knew who sat before him. But it couldn't be, he thought. Valentina was off in the Azores somewhere, married to Antonio Fero, and any child she had would not have been his..."May I look at your schedule, Joshua?" he asked, his voice cracking with emotion.

Wordlessly Joshua removed a slip of paper from his jacket pocket and passed it over. Dimitri unfolded it and pretended to study the days and times, but his eyes were glued to the name written in at the top: Joshua Dimitri Marques. "This is quite a heavy load," he said casually, but inside his heart thudded against his chest. Could this be Valentina's child? Could Joshua be his son?

"I'm willing to work hard, Dr. Maciel. You don't have to worry about me," Joshua replied. He took in the doctor's strange behavior. Dr. Maciel seemed nervous and confused. But the doctor quickly recovered and smiled at him.

"I'm sure I won't. I'm very impressed with your scores as well. I think you'll do just fine at St. Andrew's." Dimitri was rambling on like an idiot, but he didn't know what else to say. Suddenly, a thought occurred to him. "Who directed you into the medical field, Joshua? Was it your father?" he asked carefully, not wanting to give anything away by his facial expression.

A dark look passed over Joshua's features. "No, it wasn't," he said simply.

Dimitri decided to switch tactics. "Do you live in the area?" he tried.

"Yes," Joshua answered. "I only live two blocks from here."

Two blocks. Did that mean that Valentina might only be two blocks away as well? Dimitri rose from his chair and extended his hand across the massive desk. As Joshua rose to shake it, he said, "I'm going to try to lighten your caseload a little. I don't want you burning out before you've even gotten started. I'm here to guide you and counsel you in any way I can, Joshua."

Joshua nodded his thanks, and Dimitri watched him exit the study. Dimitri fell back into his seat, his legs weak and his chest tight. A knot of emotions rolled in his stomach, and a sense of impending fear worked through him. The situation seemed wholly unbelievable, and at the same time, he could only feel a sense of unease at what may yet come to pass.

Marta entered the room and, seeing the doctor in such a distraught state, she asked, "Is something wrong? What happened, Dr. Maciel?"

He looked up at her, his eyes filled with tears. "I think I just met my son," he said.

Stunned, Marta left his office, closing the door behind her, and leaving Dr. Maciel to his thoughts.

"I never thought of the possibility that I impregnated Valentina." It sounded so cold and technical to his ears, but Dimitri's shock refused to wear off. The thought of her carrying his child, all alone, shook him to his very core. There Joshua had stood before him, his son: tall, strong, his hair the color of ripened wheat. "Even now his image burns brightly in my mind," Dimitri uttered into the room. He closed his eyes to savor the remembrance.

* * *

Joshua walked home, his thoughts jumbled. Dr. Maciel had been shaken by his visit, of that he had no doubt. Why had the doctor reacted so strangely, he wondered. There was also the question of how similar they were to each other. A tiny voice nagged at him to explore the matter further, but Joshua decided to let it rest. "Just a coincidence," he muttered as he opened the gate and entered his yard. Dr. Maciel was his new boss, and that was all.

Chapter 23

Marta was not only a loyal employee, but she had taken on the role of Dimitri's surrogate mother as well after her husband died, since they had never had any children. She had dedicated herself to her work, and especially to Dr. Maciel. Lately he had been so distracted, however, and she knew it had everything to do with the new intern at the hospital. Dr. Maciel had called him his son, but he had never mentioned any children to her. He had been a bachelor for so long that she doubted he would ever marry. But this boy had somehow affected him. Was he starting to feel the effects of a life without children of his own, or was this boy really Dimitri Maciel's son? The young man did strongly resemble him…

She shook off her thoughts and readied herself for a day filled with errands. She had groceries to buy for supper, and she still had to heat the iron to press her uniform…

"Oh dear," she said aloud as she stared at the bag of trousers that waited by the front door. It was not unusual for her take or pick up the doctor's clothes from Andre's, a tailor on the other side of the city. But Andre had passed away several weeks ago, an unfortunate occurrence that had slipped Marta's mind with the upheaval of Dr. Maciel's new intern.

"What's wrong?" Dimitri had just come home from the hospital. He took one look at Marta's face and was immediately concerned.

"Nothing serious, really. But I had forgotten to tell you that Andre's is closed. He passed away several weeks ago." She looked distressed as she added, "I meant to get these pants done and forgot all about it."

"Don't trouble yourself," he reassured her. "Didn't you mention a place not far from here that now does alterations?"

Marta's face lit up. "That's right! There's a shop two blocks from here that a friend of mine recommended, but for the life of me I can't remember the name of it. I know it's in a pink Victorian house with white wicker furniture on the porch and huge colorful azaleas in the front yard. My friend said it used to be an old, gray, abandoned home, but someone bought it some years ago and took a bold step in repainting it herself." Marta chuckled as she supplied, "She's the talk of the lunch hour gossip."

"A pink house, you say?" The very idea amused him. "I think I'll be able to find it," he said as he picked up the bag. "I'll stop there in between patients this afternoon."

* * *

Dimitri walked the several blocks from the hospital to his street, then two more to the street where the shop was situated. His mind was a jumble of thoughts, most of them about Joshua. The boy was strangely tight-lipped about his family, even though Dimitri had tried to coax whatever information he could from him. But he had to admit that he worked very hard, much harder than any other intern he'd ever trained. Joshua reminded him so much of himself at that age, driven with a need to succeed.

His family had been furious when he'd decided to come to America instead of studying in Lisbon. But he needed to get as far away from his memories as possible. He'd thought that a new start in a foreign place would help him heal, but the memories had followed him there, tormenting him each time he passed a golden-haired girl on the street, or heard the strains of a well played guitar. And now Joshua opened up those wounds anew with his startling resemblance and uncanny imitation of Dimitri at the age of twenty-four. He wondered if the boy might have made any connection yet between him and his father, or if he even knew the truth. Antonio Fero had stolen that away from him, and he had been helpless to prevent it.

Dimitri stopped suddenly and grinned as he saw that the stately Victorian was in fact painted a shockingly bright pink. Obviously the owner was trying to make a statement, and if the steady stream of customers he watched entering and leaving the shop was any indication, she had good business sense as well. "Good for her," he thought as he opened the gate and walked up the driveway to the house.

He was so absorbed in studying the details of the old Victorian that he missed the "Valentina's Bridal Shop" sign hanging above the door. He peeked through the windows before stepping inside and was amazed that he had lived in the area for years and had never walked down this street before. With one hand to his forehead to shield the sun, he pressed his face to the main display window and took in the bridal gowns set up there. Blindly reaching for the handle, he again missed the sign over the door and stepped inside.

Dimitri stood in the foyer, impressed with the layout. The shop was designed to appeal mostly to women with the beautiful and elaborate bridal gowns that were strategically placed throughout the elegant space. But in one corner of the room a sign announced that all types of alterations were now done there as well. He walked up to the counter and removed his trousers from the bag. Just as he lifted his head he glimpsed an outline so achingly familiar that he stood frozen in place for a moment, his heart pounding so hard against his ribs that he thought it might burst right through his chest. "Dear God," he whispered. He turned and looked. After all these years, Valentina stood before him. He felt a twitch inside. Something he had buried years ago came alive. He fought for control, but he was getting dizzy and weak in the knees. How could he still love her so much after all these years? Every nerve ending came to life as he stared at her, his eyes never leaving hers. Pent up feelings clamored to explode within him, but as he tried to speak the words got trapped in his throat. Twenty-four years had gone by, but the intimacy they'd shared had them locked in this moment of time.

Valentina moved first, closing the distance between them. She walked as if in a trance, unwilling to believe that Dimitri stood before her. It could not be true. But as she came closer, he reached for her first, and lifted her hand to his lips. He closed his eyes as he kissed the back of it, and she had to turn away sharply as tears suddenly fell down her cheeks. "I'm sorry," she said. "I didn't mean to cry."

He lifted his head, and she saw that he was crying too. Without a word he took her head in his hands, their eyes locked together. Bringing her face up to his, he claimed a kiss that had hung like a promise over them for decades. With their mouths still joined, he reached for her hair and sought out the pins that held it bound. He removed each one until her curls cascaded down her back, just as he remembered them.

"Let me look at you," she managed to say when they at last broke their kiss. Dimitri's hair was darker than she remembered. It was neatly parted to one side, but his face was the mold of their son's. They held each other again tightly. Valentina felt like she was eighteen again.

He caught her studying his face and said quietly, "You married the wrong man, Valentina."

"I know, Dimitri," she replied. She took a deep breath and decided that he had to know the truth now, while she still had the nerve to tell him. "I have something special to tell you," she said. "We have a son."

"Joshua," Dimitri whispered.

"How did you know?" she asked, bewildered.

"He works for me, Valentina. He's the new intern at the hospital where I work. I knew the moment I saw him that he was our son." Dimitri tried to keep his voice steady, but he could barely maintain his composure. It had been one thing to suspect Joshua's parentage. It was another to have Valentina confirm it.

"I'd wanted to tell you, Dimitri, so many times. Ever since he was a child Joshua spoke of becoming a doctor. I had hoped he would turn out to be as noble as you, and he did. You will be so proud of him." Valentina watched Dimitri's face for a reaction, any reaction, but he seemed so far away that she thought her news had angered him.

Shocked and taken aback that his suspicions had been confirmed, Dimitri replied in a weak voice, "Why didn't you tell me the truth, Valentina? You decided all on your own that I would leave you pregnant and unwed. You made the decision that it was better to leave than to face the villagers and whatever they might think of you. Was your pride bigger than our love?" he demanded.

She took hold of his hands, and with a deep sigh told Dimitri her story with no detail omitted. "I was young and foolish, Dimitri. And yes, I was too naive for my own good. Your mother invited me to your house and told me that Sour Face had caught us in the orchard the night we first made love." She closed her eyes, sadness filling her as she revealed the depth of his family's hatred of her. "Your mother threatened my life if I were to stay. She guessed I was pregnant, and said that your family would never accept a bastard child. She also told me of your betrothed in Lisbon, of the pre-arranged marriage to your distant cousin. Your parents were raised to believe that status, accomplishments, and a last name were the most important considerations for a marriage."

"My God, Valentina. I never knew." Dimitri's anger raged within him. How could his mother have been so calculating? "There was no marriage, or even a cousin for that matter. It was all lies."

Valentina stepped back as anger and bewilderment raged within. It had all been a lie. Mrs. Maciel had just wanted her out of the picture. She took a deep and steadying breath. "Now do you understand why it was so difficult to say anything? I fell in love with you, but the only thing that mattered to them was that I carried a bastard child. My life has not been easy. I lived with a man who kept me under lock and key, afraid my shame would rub off on the other girls in the village. It was so hard to live with the whispers of 'It's not Antonio's baby she carries. Add up the months and see for yourself.' And when Joshua was born, he looked nothing like a Fero, and barely even resembled me. I wanted to curl up and die, but as time passed I became stronger. Your family would never have accepted our baby or me. I make no excuses for my life or how I've lived it, but my struggle carved me into the woman I am today, and I will not be ashamed of that."

A part of him understood what Valentina meant, but he could not help asking, "So you didn't come to me because you feared my mother more than you loved me?"

Valentina backed away from him, her expression unreadable. She replied, "I was eighteen years old and yes, I was scared. I thought you might understand what I went through, but I can see that you don't. I think it's better if you leave, Dimitri." It hurt so much to say that to him, but Valentina was not the naïve girl she once was. She was far stronger than she had ever thought she could be, and no man, not even Dimitri, would take from her what she had fought so hard to win.

It was difficult for both of them to find parting words. Dimitri, hurt by Valentina's betrayal of their love, walked backwards toward the door, saying, "I need time to absorb all of this." He put his hand on the door handle and opened it, walking out without a glance back.

Valentina watched him go, a single thought replaying itself in her head. "Funny how everyone needs time to adjust," she said aloud. "My time was always taken away." But she was now faced with another awkward situation. She had to tell Joshua that the man he worked for was his father, if he did not already suspect it. She feared his reaction to the news. They had not spoken of his father since he'd returned home, and she suspected it was because he had not come to terms yet with his anger and resentment. What would he say now when he learned that he had been working with his father all this time?

She shuddered as the realization of what just happened finally hit her. Dimitri had come back into her life after all these years, but their reunion had not gone at all like she had imagined it might. He was angry, bitter, and she knew he had a right to be. But she would not let him undermine what she had spent so many years trying to strengthen. Her whole life had been a series of struggles, and she would not sacrifice the independence she now enjoyed for a man who could not see the love she still had for him.

* * *

Dimitri went away with a wounded heart and remembrance of his youth. The love he felt for Valentina was ever so present. He couldn't forget. All those nights that he used to wake up in the darkness, he would stretch out his arm in search of her, thinking she was near. At times he would actually imagine he felt the silken brush of her hair on his face or the scent of the fresh, soapy smell of her skin. The dull pain would again begin to thud against his chest wall. Every night he would close his eyes and see her image, remembering that hot summer night. He knew he'd fallen in love with her but he hadn't known she would change his life forever. He somehow found his way home, unlocked the front door and went straight to his study. Dimitri fell into his chair and rested his head on his arms on top of the desk.

Valentina was here, in the city, and only two blocks away. But she might as well have been back in the Azores. He had imagined what a reunion with her might be like over a thousand times, but he'd never pictured it like this. Their long held love for each other had been overshadowed by the ugly truths of the past. And now there was the added shock of his son. He had suspected strongly, but now, to be sure…

"I've missed you so much," he said into the empty room. "Now that we've found each other again, can we make it work?"

Unable to answer his own question, Dimitri wept quietly until he fell into a light, dreamless sleep.

Chapter 24

Joshua walked home with hurried steps. He was tired after working a twelve hour shift, and all he wanted to do was go home and go to bed. He was glad to see his mother had not locked up the shop for the night. He could walk in the front door since it was the quickest way to his room. He stopped short when he saw his mother sitting in the foyer, waiting for him. "Mother, I'm glad you're still up," he said. "I had the most amazing afternoon."

"What happened?" she asked. Inside, Valentina was a bundle of nerves. She had to tell Joshua about Dimitri's visit, but he was so obviously excited over what had happened to him today that she remained silent. "Tell me what happened," she encouraged.

Joshua began to pace. His eyes were shining with pride as he explained. "I had the most exciting experience at the hospital. A young girl about seventeen came in today, ready to give birth. She was all alone, no family or friends to support her. She reminded me a little of you, Mother. She was so scared. Dr. Maciel was called in and he had me hold her hand as she pushed. I looked into her eyes and saw the fear and uncertainty there, and I understood what it must have been like for you all those years ago.

"The labor was long and very difficult. Finally, after the baby's head started to crown, Dr. Maciel announced it wouldn't be long now and called me to his side to guide the baby out. He guided my hands in supporting and turning the baby's head as it emerged into the world."

Valentina felt her heart constrict at the image of her son and his father together, bringing a new life into the world. *This is why I fought so hard for you,* she acknowledged as tears threatened to fall. "What happened next?" she asked gently.

"She gave birth to a baby girl." Joshua's earlier tiredness was forgotten as he remembered the surge of energy that had raced through him when he delivered that baby into the world. "Even before she was bathed and wrapped, her mother felt this wet little bundle on her belly, reached down to the naked baby and touched her blood streaked, capped little black head. As she stroked the baby's soft hair, she whispered, 'I can't.'

"I asked her what she meant, and she gazed up at me with the most serene expression I have ever seen. 'I was going to give her up for adoption,' she explained. 'But I took one look at her, and realized that I can't do it. I can't give my baby away. I loved her from the moment I knew she was inside of me, and it was that love that kept me going all these months, even after my family threw me out of my house and I was forced to go live with the nuns on the other side of town. I prayed that my baby would have a good home when she was born, but her home is with me. Thank you,' she said as the tears poured from her eyes. 'You've given me a wonderful gift.'

"I didn't know what to say. They took the baby away to be cleaned up and dressed, and Dr. Maciel was called away to another patient. I just stood there and let it all sink in. I'd never delivered a baby before. I'd seen it all in my books and had been taught all of the mechanics of it through my professors' lectures, but to feel that tiny life in my hands, to understand just what it meant to feel real joy..." Joshua wiped at his eyes as several tears escaped down his cheeks. "It really hit me, Mother, the moment of my own birth, the happiness and disappointment of it all. I felt the pain of not knowing how that girl would survive, but I also knew the profound love she had for her baby. Just like you."

Valentina looked up at her son with pride, and found in him the blessing that had accompanied her throughout her struggles. "Joshua," she said, "my mother tried to curb my rebellious ways when I was only seventeen too. She gave me the rules of moral behavior, what was right and what was wrong." Valentina chuckled as she went on. "I wasn't influenced by traditions, and in the process I fell in love. I'm not sorry for the result. Fate separated your father and me, but I've kept his image alive in my memory with the passage of time."

"It's all right, Mother," Joshua reassured her. "You taught me how to grow beyond my own limits, and you taught me to respect another person's independent existence. Even through your feelings of hopelessness and aloneness, you dared to dream. Because of that, you have security and status in the community. I just hope that young girl will realize that she can do the same for herself, and not give in to despair," he sighed.

"You could have given me up for adoption, or put me in an orphanage. I could have been raised in a home of bitterness and lies, and my emotional life could have been a tangled mess."

He looked thoughtful as he said, "I treat people for fractured bones and all sorts of other ailments, but I'm unable to fix a fractured soul. That girl taught me something today. Mother, you have a deep wound, but even with the passing of time it's only partially healed. Your life consists of lonely days and empty nights." He bent and kissed his mother's cheek. "Thank you for unlocking your heart and sharing your sense of right and wrong with me. I saw you in that girl today, and I finally understood what you've been trying to tell me."

Joshua began to climb the stairs, ready for a good night's sleep.

"I need to tell you something," Valentina called softly.

She was tense with emotion and he immediately went to her. "Mother, what's wrong?" he asked.

Valentina looked into his eyes, Dimitri's eyes. She had to tell him. She had fought with herself over this all afternoon, but hearing Joshua's story made her think he might be able to handle her revelation, and there was no other option available now. Dimitri knew, and soon the news would reach her son. But she wanted to tell him first. "You know most of the bits and pieces of my complicated life, Joshua, but tonight I have one last piece to share with you. Dr. Maciel visited the shop today."

"My boss?" asked Joshua. "Am I in trouble?" he joked, but he instantly sobered at his mother's solemn expression.

Just tell him. "Dr. Maciel is your father, Joshua. At first I couldn't believe it," she quickly added as she took in Joshua's dumbstruck expression. "When you'd told me his name, I'd thought it was a strange coincidence and brushed it off. But after this afternoon…I don't know what else to say."

"My father?" His expression was instantly defiant as he replied disapprovingly, "I don't believe it."

But he knew in his heart it was true. His mother's pained expression verified her words. She raised a hand to her mouth and said, "I've made a real mess of things, haven't I?"

Joshua simply reached for her and they held each other as they both cried. "I am so proud of you, Joshua. You've shown me what a good, upstanding man you have become with your actions today. Please don't let this destroy what you've worked so hard to achieve," she sobbed.

Joshua pulled away from her and tried to smile. "I stood next to him all afternoon, Mother, and he never said a word. I delivered a child today with my fa-father's help," he choked out. Joshua helped his mother to her feet and hugged her. "It's all right. Let's just get some sleep and figure this all out tomorrow."

* * *

But the memory of that awkward moment kept Joshua up all night. He could not sleep after he learned that Dr. Maciel was his father. He was tormented by the revelation, but strangely not all that surprised. As he thought about his first meeting with Dr. Maciel, certain things clicked into place: his shocked expression at meeting Joshua, the probing questions. The good doctor must have known or at least suspected. At the time, Joshua just brushed the coincidences off, but perhaps he should not have been so hasty. At first he was startled with the look on the doctor's face. He now knew that it was a sign of recognition, that when Dr. Maciel looked at Joshua, he was staring into his own face. *And what would you have done?* his conscience argued.

"How do I approach this delicate situation?" he wondered out loud as he watched the clock tick by painstakingly slow. But at the same time he was anxious to confront what would not doubt be a very uncomfortable situation as well. Dr. Maciel had started out as his tutor, and was now his father.

To leave the hospital now and asked to be reassigned would be failure in his own eyes, but it was more than that. His deeper conflict lay in his real fear of displaying any tender emotions towards this man who he had come to like and respect. He also knew that after confronting Dr. Maciel, there would be many awkward days ahead and his strength would be tested. With the frozen truth of the past out in the open, Joshua knew there would be an argument for reconciliation. "But I don't know if I'm ready for that," he admitted to himself. He had tried very hard to see his mother's side in all of this, to understand why she'd done what she had, and why Dr. Maciel might not have been at fault for what happened to his family. *Then why am I so angry?* He tossed and turned on that thought for a while before he fell into a troubled sleep.

* * *

Joshua marched straight into Dr. Maciel's office. He needed to get this off his chest before the day started and the doctor started seeing patients. Sensing someone in the doorway, Dimitri looked up from his paperwork and there stood Joshua Dimitri Marques, his son. The boy did not have a smile on his face the way he usually did first thing in the morning. His expression was hard, and Dimitri was again struck by how much Joshua resembled him.

"I want to tell you how I feel about you," Joshua spat out. He took a shaky breath and forged ahead, heedless of the consequences. "I might be a bastard child but I'm not a coward like you. I would fight for the woman I loved."

Dimitri rose from his chair and walked around it to rest his hands on its back. He needed to put some distance between them. "I didn't know she was pregnant," he replied quietly.

With a look of outrage Joshua shot back, "But you knew how to use her body to satisfy your selfish desires, didn't you! You could have gone public with your love for her so people would have accepted the idea that you loved one another. But after using her you just hid behind the secured gates of your expensive house. And because life had become so ugly and unbearable, my mother was forced to flee her home."

Joshua shut the door behind him and slumped into the chair in front of the desk. Weary, he continued. "It was determination in molding my destiny that dictated which course of action my mother took. In life you need love and security, but you gave her neither." He regarded Dr. Maciel a moment. "You know, maybe if you let your pride admit your weakness, we could all move forward."

Dimitri lifted a hand, palm out, and said, "That's enough. You may have my features, but you have your mother's impulsive nature, and that was my weakness. I loved her so much that I let her have her way all the time. You said I was too proud to admit my weakness. I want you to know that yes, I was weak and immature then. I failed to take a stand with your mother and do everything in my power to stop her marriage. I lost out in the end. She was blessed in having you for a son, and I'm not too proud to humble myself before you and tell you how proud I am to be your father. If you give me a chance to be a part of your life, I'll prove to you that I have a mature understanding of the word love. You're right, Joshua. We do have choices in life. Your mother took a giant leap of faith by crossing the waters of the Atlantic Ocean on a hope and a prayer of a promising future."

Joshua sat silently, absorbing every word. Dimitri came around the desk and leaned against the front. He looked down at his son and said, "As I look back on my life, I would have done things differently. I always suspected my mother had a hand in all of this, but I had no proof. I heard the whispered rumors that she was glad never to lay eyes on your mother again after she went away, and I learned of her dislike for Valentina. I moved on with my life, not in the direction my parents hoped for me, and I haven't had any contact with them in twenty-five years. You lived the first twenty-four years of your life with one parent. I have lived the past twenty-five years of mine with none. Because of my love for your mother, I never married. When I saw her for the first time after all these years, she took my breath away, just as she always had."

Dimitri paused before his next statement, careful to choose his words with care. "Son," he said gently, his voice filled with pride, "your emotions are tender right now. Give it all a chance to sink in, but don't turn me away, please." He extended his arms, unsure of how Joshua might react.

Joshua rose and walked into his father's embrace, tears spilling from his relieved eyes. "Together we'll adjust," Dimitri reassured Joshua as he hugged him close. "We'll share

in the blessings of growth."

"I don't know how to do that," Joshua choked out, "but I'm willing to try. For my mother's sake, I will do the best I can."

"I know, son, I know. We'll try for each other too. I've missed out on a great deal, but not anymore." Dimitri held his son and let his own tears fall freely.

Chapter 25

Days had passed and Valentina wondered if Dimitri would return. The clock chimed seven and she was glad to close up the shop for the night. She had watched the door each day, hoping he might come and talk to her again. Joshua had remained quiet about Dimitri and work, though she knew her son would have confronted him by now. But she was grateful that he did not seem as angry as he once had. He had in fact encouraged her to visit him at the hospital. For some strange reason she believed Joshua wanted her to see Dimitri again, but she would not chase after him like a love struck schoolgirl. He knew where she lived. If he wanted to see her, he would have to come here.

She found herself looking at the display mannequin with her trademark white bridal gown draped over it, a trailing veil adorning its head. Would she ever get the chance to wear it? She dared not think of the possibility. She'd gotten her hopes up before, but she wouldn't allow herself to do that again. She allowed herself to reflect on her life for a moment, and wondered if she had made the right choice when she let Dimitri go all those years ago. She finally understood the origin of her impulsiveness, the need she had for independence and freedom of thought. But she chose wrongly when it came to Dimitri and the life they could have had together. His return forced her to face the ghosts of her past, ghosts she had hoped were locked in an unremembered chamber of her heart. She spent years guilt-ridden with fantasies and dreams of her lost love, and now he had miraculously returned, only to have those same ghosts prevent their love once more.

It was too much for a weary soul to bear. Valentina sighed and locked the front door, going about her nightly routine as she prepared to say good night to her mother.

* * *

Dimitri tried the front door of the shop, but it was locked. He walked around the back of the house to the kitchen door, and found it opened halfway. He pulled open the screen door and stepped inside. The small kitchen was cool and well lived in. Bread and a butter knife sat on a small table, and other odds and ends marked this as Valentina's kitchen. He heard voices from the hallway beyond, and recognized Valentina saying good night to her mother. He moved closer to the door and watched her come down the hall, her back straight and her hair neatly pinned up in a tight bun. He was crazy just to walk in on her like this, but he was desperate to see her, and if this was the way he had to do it, then so be it.

* * *

Valentina stopped as she heard a noise from the kitchen. Joshua was not due home for another hour. She then remembered that the back door was open, and feared thieves had entered the house. She gasped as a man suddenly appeared in the hallway. "I'm so sorry, Valentina," said a tired and raspy voice. "I've been such a fool."

Valentina stepped back in surprise. Was her mind playing tricks on her? "Dimitri?" she called out.

Dimitri emerged from the shadows of the hallway. He looked worn and haggard, and he had dark circles under his eyes. They stared at each other in silence, then Valentina closed the distance between them. She threw her arms around his neck and with a faint cry, exclaimed, "I was hoping you'd come back!"

"Never thought to come find me, did you?" he teased. They kissed long and deeply, the years of their separation a distant memory as they held each other close.

Valentina pulled away from him and removed the pins from her hair, letting it flow loosely around her. Dimitri could not resist and he ran his hand down the length of her hair. "I've carried a torch for you all these years," he said as he pulled her into his arms and inhaled her sweet fragrance. "That's why I never married. No one had ever measured up to you."

Valentina started to cry. She felt his strength and the trembling in him as she stepped back into his embrace. "I waited up for you that night in my house." It seemed like another lifetime ago. "I'd made a dress just for you, and I was going to tell you about Joshua. I thought you had come in the door, but I looked up and it was Antonio." She wiped her eyes and choked out, "After the rape, I felt soiled and I thought you'd never want to touch me again. And I felt rejected when you stayed away from me."

"I can't tell you enough how sorry I am," he said, his arms wrapped securely around her. "You've had a lifetime to adjust to all of this. I know I've been unfair. I just needed these last few days to reevaluate my life and where we could go from here."

He pulled away from her and reached for her hand. In a hurried voice he said, "Please come with me. I have something to show you." They left the house and headed for the street, walking and talking as if they didn't have a care in the world. Valentina felt like she was eighteen again as she held onto Dimitri's hand. She felt light, carefree, as if the years of sorrow had not occurred at all, and the beginning of her life was this very moment.

"Where are we going?" she asked as they stopped before a large house. It reminded her of the old woman's house back in *Arrifes*.

"Here," he replied as he opened the gate. "This is my house."

He took her face in his hands and said, "My God, I love you so much. I am halfway through my life, and I had given up hope of ever loving you again, but then I found you. Come." He took her hand and led her around to the back of the house. "I want you to see the backyard," he added cryptically.

Valentina put a hand to her mouth in surprise. "Oh my! It's an orchard!"

"Not just an orchard," he explained, "but a replica of Sour Face's, with all the curved paths, just like the place where we made love, surrounded by the orange trees under the stars."

She took it all in, the graceful, flowing trees laden with ripe crab apples and pears in the middle of New York. It seemed impossible, but she couldn't deny the miracle before her. The blueberries that lined the path were just as she remembered. He'd captured all of the details, just as they had been twenty-four years before.

"Dimitri." Valentina held his hand to her heart and spoke the words she had never thought to say again. "I love you now more than ever."

He gathered her close and kissed her, his lips tasting her neck, her face, any place he could reach. Their mouths met and their kiss was full of remembrance. Valentina pulled away, her breathing labored, and said, "You taste exactly the way I remembered."

Dimitri reached for her, his hands exploring every inch of her. She gasped as she felt his hands on her breasts, a touch so unexpected yet familiar that she circled his neck with her arms and kissed him, giving him permission to love her.

He wasted no time. He ran his hands along her body as he drank deeply of her. She could feel his desire for her, and in a frenzy they shed their clothes and lay together on the soft grass. "It hurt so much to watch you leave me," he murmured as he kissed her slowly. "I thought distance and time would help me forget and I could move on, but I could never forget you."

He kissed her again and touched her in places he had loved many years ago. She too touched him and made him tremble with need. Their joining was swift and passionate, and when they reached the limits of their desire, he said in a voice filled with tenderness, "I've missed you."

"I've missed you too," she whispered.

"Then marry me. I never want to be away from you again."

"Yes," she answered softly.

He took her on the same journey of their youth, where they had so long ago explored each other's innocence. Now they shared in a journey of spirit as well as bodies.

"My mother once said that if you're ever touched by love, that love multiplies just as you give it. Our love has only grown over the years. Time and separation haven't dimmed it," Valentina whispered as the night sky gave way to the soft shades of dawn.

"Did I ever tell you that your mother is a very wise woman?" Dimitri replied as he gently kissed her shoulder.

Valentina laughed as his mouth covered hers, and they shared in their love once more.

* * *

Valentina wore her signature dress with its flowing veil, designed so long ago and at last worn to her own wedding, a marriage to the man she loved more than anything in the world. Dimitri stood proudly, his hands joined in front of him. Joshua stood by his side, a grin spread wide across his face. She marveled at the striking resemblance between her soon to be husband and her son. It was like looking into a mirror. She tried but failed to hold back her tears as she slowly made her way down the aisle. Her mother wiped at her own tears as Valentina walked by her. Her sister and brother-in-law smiled broadly, while Gabriela gave her a wave and Augusto graced her with a wink. Even John and Miguel had come to New York to share in her special day. She had not lost her friends after all, but gained a family she could never have imagined. And as she made her way to the front of the church, she knew she had at last come home.

* * *

Dimitri watched Valentina approach, and knew his family circle was now complete, just as the round golden rings that would seal their vows symbolized the closing of a circle. He never thought to see Valentina again, but here she was, about to become his wife. "I love you," he whispered as he took her hand.

"I love you," she replied with a smile.

The ceremony was short but full of meaning, and the priest's words resounded throughout the church: "God bless you both on this very special day, and every day of your lives. With marriage comes change and growth, but if you can come together in both happiness and fears, you will share the gift of bonding that marriage brings."

When the ceremony ended Valentina and Dimitri looked at each other and exclaimed together, "We're married!"

"Yes you are," Joshua said as he hugged both his parents. "It's about time."

Epilogue

Valentina strolled through the orchard, a pleased smile on her lips. She reached up and was about to pluck an apple loose when a deep voice behind her demanded, "What do you think you're doing?"

"Just stealing an orange." It was as if they had stepped back in time, and she really was trying to steal and orange off the old woman's tree. The fact that she stood in the middle of New York with an apple in her hand was irrelevant. She spun around and her eyes settled on Dimitri, his own eyes sparkling with amusement. He stepped towards her and she said, "You're right. The oranges in your orchard are better than Sour Face's."

"I know." He pulled her into his arms and gazed down at her. "But I also remember telling you that you'd have to trade me a kiss for an orange any time you wanted one," he reminded her as he too recalled their conversation from long ago.

"So you did. And since I want an orange…" She cupped his face with her hands and brought his lips to hers. The sweet, familiar taste of him made Valentina's heart sing. It was impossible and all too real at the same time. All these years, and after so much pain and misfortune, here she was, wrapped in the arms of the only man she'd ever loved.

"I'll give you two oranges for that one," Dimitri teased as they broke their kiss. He let his gaze linger on the soft, golden waves of her hair, her sparkling green eyes and inviting lips. "I'm so happy, Valentina," he confided quietly as he placed a light kiss on her forehead.

"So am I." She was Mrs. Dimitri Maciel now. For the first time in her life, Valentina felt whole, complete. Nothing mattered anymore except the feel of her husband in her arms and the knowledge that she was very blessed indeed.

"What are you thinking about?" Dimitri asked as he brushed a stray curl from her face.

"I was thinking about how much I love you," she answered, her lips again finding his.

"Me too," he replied between their kisses. "Me too."

Also available from PublishAmerica

SLEEP TIGHT

by Barbara Wagner

Paperback, 289 pages
6″ x 9″
ISBN 1-60610-096-3

Attractive Caryl Stewart, a western artist, has inherited a fortune and fallen in love with David Eagle, the confident and sensual man of her dreams. When her flamboyant, oil-rich great-aunt, Savannah Buckman, dies, the young redhead travels from Scottsdale, Arizona, to manage her great-aunt's estate in upscale Winter Park near Oklahoma City. After a disturbing secret from Savannah's past is revealed and a manipulative friend, almost Caryl's exact twin, becomes the third victim, Caryl knows she is the target of a cunning killer, an unknown murderer who is slowly going insane. Tormented by Oklahoma wind and trapped in the eerie atmosphere of a mysterious mansion, she struggles to escape from a maze of terror, revenge and murder. When her Native American lover is accused, Caryl makes a startling discovery and a cruel psychopath prepares to combine her death with his pleasure.

About the author:

Both a writer and an artist, Barbara Wagner lives with her husband in a suburb of Kansas City close to their grown children. She grew up in Oklahoma, has a degree in fine art from the University of Oklahoma, and studied creative writing at Butler University in Indianapolis. An award-winning artist, her work was marketed in Scottsdale, Arizona, for many years. Though *Sleep Tight* is entirely a work of fiction, the artistic life of the novel's protagonist, Caryl Stewart, is drawn from Barbara's own experience and adds a strong framework to the suspenseful story.

Available to all bookstores nationwide.
www.publishamerica.com

Also available from PublishAmerica

EMILLEE KART AND THE SEVEN SAVING SIGNS

THE TALE OF BEASLEY'S BONNET

by Vanessa Wheeler

Paperback, 202 pages
5.5″ x 8.5″
ISBN 1-4241-8597-1

From the minute she met her eccentric missionary aunt, Emillee Kart's life would never be the same. During their first lunch at the Butterfly Café, Emillee is inducted into a secret club known as the Monarch's Army; minutes later she is running for her life. Not only is Emillee launched into an age-old battle between the Skywalkers and the Hexiums, she may very well be the key to saving the Earthtreadors. Twelve years ago, on the day Emillee was born, a prophecy spread throughout the land of a child that would turn the tide of the battle. Five children were born on that day; two have disappeared. The Hexiums will stop at nothing to eliminate any threat to their victory. Emillee needs to learn who she is in order to help uncover the clues that will bring the Skywalkers closer to their goal.

About the author:

Love of fantasy combined with spiritual conviction guided this mother of three to spin this faith- based tale. Joanne Strobel-Cort, born in Bethlehem, Pennsylvania, now lives in Summit, New Jersey, with her husband and three children. She works on Wall Street and is a committed Sunday school teacher who relies on faith to meet the challenges of each day.

Available to all bookstores nationwide.
www.publishamerica.com